A Suit For Melvin

Jo E. Jennings

ISBN: 9798818866833

TABLE OF CONTENTS

1957: SAVING A LIFE

J.J., hater of snakes, slowed on his way home from Lake Loretta to avoid one in the center of the road: yellow, black, coiled and content.

J.J. had nothing else to do but hurry home, hoping food smells were coming from his grandma's apartment if she didn't have to work late at the hotel.

Called the boy with the gifted tongue by his teachers, J.J. was a seller of wieners and artichoke hearts door-to-door, drawing a festive picture, one that no woman could resist. He wasn't beyond pulling a recipe or two out of his pockets, cut from the pages of a library magazine.

If a lady weren't planning a party when he knocked, she was soon shopping for fancy napkins and getting out her fine china.

J.J. studied the current problem, circling the colorful pile of coils with curious caution.

"I don't suppose you're *the* snake," he said, "the one that made the two people eat fruit?"

The snake ignored him, which suited J.J. just fine. No use to rattle a snake, so as to cause its devil tongue to appear and threaten. Get it? Rattle? You rattling the snake instead of the snake rattling you?

J.J. scanned the road. Traffic had been light as he'd searched the woods for a fishing hole, although he had no pole. It was just something to do.

He didn't want the creature to die, but it was too *snaky* to nonchalantly pick up, as big as a half dollar. OK, maybe a quarter.

It was difficult to tell the exact size since it was rolled up like a fire hose. Was it hiding something under all those coils? Snakes always look so secretive.

J.J. chose a river-bottom stone, holding it to his lips.

"This is J.J. Baskin coming to you from Small Town, Mo.," he said, making certain to emphasize that the last syllable of Missouri was pronounced as an *a*. His grandmother had often noted that if Missouri were meant to be pronounced Missour–ee, it would have ended in *ie*. It did not.

"Zo-ol-o-gists have come from the world over to solve the mystery of this creature on the ledge of death," J.J. continued.

"Passersby shudder in their pursuit to protect this reptile from oncoming traffic. . ."

"I know I'm exaggerating or right-out lying, but I'm making a better story," J.J. said to no one in particular unless he had the ear of God.

Who could be certain?

Interesting concept, ear of God.

"Mr. Stripe," he said, "this is a stupid place to lie. Mrs. Stripe has a raw egg all laid out for your supper, and the little Stripes are waiting for you. You could be lots flatter and a whole lot wider. You'll have the whole family in knots—get it? in knots? . . . a snake in knots?"

"Your mother-in-law will claim she knew all along you'd become roadkill. Hmmm. Heard that one before, have you? Me, too."

A kaleidoscope of lights caught a ride on a breeze, hang-gliding through polka-dot spots among the leaves, leaking patches of blue down on J.J. when he looked up, but reflecting shadow freckles when he looked down.

A breeze rippled his tousled curly hair, sending shivers up his bare legs.

No answers spilled down from the overflow dam, so he waited for a miracle to appear, knowing snakes -- at least serpents as they were called – or asps -- had rubbed God the wrong way a long time ago.

The scene from the leafy chapel where he stood resembled a dime store oil painting, colors blurred in with an occasional flower, a tiny house in the distance probably owned by some lady who baked ginger-bread, maybe even with raisins.

There was hardly a sound except for the sporadic flop of a fish in the water or the buzz of something fuzzy flying by.

Planes were humming thousands of miles away, strips of soundless ribbons in the sky.

"One thing we don't get in this small town is talking snakes except maybe at the tent churches in summer. Grandma says the snakes don't really talk, that the people claiming they do have been drinking whiskey out behind the tent."

He peered off down the road.

No cars.

"Last week I climbed up on the school roof. This is a true story. I'm not as tall as the other seventh graders," J. J. chattered.

"Short people get a lot of dares. So, I did that on a dare."

He touched the snake softly with his bare big toe, not enough for a response. He couldn't say what it felt like – dry maybe.

It didn't move.

"I'd really hate to see you made into a wall hanging – or a belt," he said to the reptile. "No self-respecting snake should end its life with its ends held together around a big 'ol belly by a rodeo buckle."

3

Suddenly recognizing a house on the other side of the lake, J.J. started to run.

"If you want to get out of the road while I'm gone, do, but in case you don't, I'm going for help," he shouted.

Everyone at school knew the house by the lake was Melvin Beasley's, home of the skeleton boy and the so-called 11 children.

Eleven? No one ever saw them except at school, and then who was to know if they were counting the same five or six over and over again.

They looked alike except for the oldest one, and even he had some likeness. He was just bigger, probably could grab food off the table faster than the little ones, accounting for his size.

No one would consider painting Melvin's house for a dime store picture with a frame, and even then, it looked too much like a witch's house, so no one would want to buy it.

J.J. himself lived over the drug store in town, and he knew his magazines. Melvin's house was a *SATURDAY EVENING POST* photo; yet, he had a backyard and all the trees anyone could dream of having.

An old hound lay panting outside a disheveled dog house, the only movement outside the shack except for the clothes blowing on the clothesline.

One more child in the yard wasn't going to make this xylophone-ribbed dog bark.

The dog would ignore J.J., just like the kids at school never paid attention to Melvin Beasley.

There were stories suggesting he was a skeleton come to life.

Melvin had always been quiet and predictable like a desk, never missing school, not saying one word. He'd never even had chicken pox.

He wore farmer's overalls and tattered, ragged shoes, sometimes with his toes sticking out the leather, covered with a rag. In warm weather he wore nothing under his overalls, and in the winter, he just wore long-johns underneath, no shirt.

His underwear or skin had been showing for so many winters and summers that unless there were a new kid at school, no one giggled any more.

Melvin's head was almost bald, the results of bloody home haircuts, clippers too close to the scalp in spots.

He probably didn't have enough spirit to say, "Ouch."

One side of his lip curled so that his teeth showed even when his mouth was closed.

Melvin gazed with no dreams, rolling with the ups and downs over rocks, bugs, and frogs like a leaf in a stream.

The kids made jokes about Melvin in front of him as if his feelings were in a cave somewhere.

On Valentine's Day, Melvin's Valentines never came out of the sack if anyone remembered to give him one.

As J.J. ran toward the shack by the lake, he remembered Halloween, how Melvin sat stiff and dead-like, wearing a Cream-of-Wheat box front over his face, two holes cut out for eyes and two for strings which held the box to his face.

The kids pointed at Melvin, shouting, "What are *you* supposed to be?"

He curled up in his desk like a sow bug, pulling in his arms and legs, rolling into a ball of sorts.

It wouldn't have been as depressing if Melvin hadn't made an effort.

He had endeavored to be like them, and it fizzled the first time.

If Melvin had been clever, putting a towel around his shoulders, standing on the desk shouting, "I'm Cream-of-Wheat-man," the kids would have bought that.

He may have even won a prize.

But he was just the skeleton boy with a cereal box over his face, a strange mask held on with two strings.

J.J. 's own costume was made of wonderful material scraps, and he'd won an orange-flavored sucker shaped like a jack-o-lantern.

He'd taken until Christmas to lick off the white face and still had the stick in his underwear drawer.

"Melvin is just poor," he thought. There was no shame in being poor as long as you were clean. That's what J.J.'s grandmother said.

Melvin was—clean enough.

J.J. was now running toward Melvin's house to save a snake.

What if he never came out alive?

What if the family wanted to use J.J. for food?

J.J. shivered.

Even the idea of seeing the inside of the standing-room-only shack sounded scary, but J.J. had left the gravel road for the cool grass by Melvin's house, weeds-gone-to-seed tickling his ankles, burrs poking at him.

He knocked timidly on the door, fearful it would fall in. A tiny desolate face peeked out at him, with round staring brown eyes.

"*What-chew-want?*"

"Tell Melvin it's a friend from school," he said, his pride at stake.

"*Melvin's scott-no-friends.*"

"You're wrong; he's got me," J.J. said.

There was no shout of, "MELLLVIN"!

The little girl backed up, making a space one-and-a-half-Melvin's wide.

The children sat on the floor around the mother, who sat holding a catalog beneath a single bulb dangling from the ceiling.

"Could I speak with Melvin please?" J.J. asked politely, despite the smell of vinegar and dirty feet.

He tried not to goggle at the rags strewn around -- for beds he supposed. Did they each have a rag bed, or at night did they all scramble for a spot?

There was a portable cupboard but no obvious cook stove. A tin wash pan hung from a hook of a pot-bellied contraption.

Melvin's mother and the pretty little girl who answered the door were the only ones without a curled lip. Maybe Melvin's mom would have been beautiful without the bruised eyes which were almost swollen shut.

J.J. was hypnotized by the round, hard belly on her frail body, protecting another baby inside.

He wished someone could say to him, "Here, J.J., put your hand right here and feel your brother kick."

"My children don't go out," the mother said kindly.

"I don't want to play," J.J. explained. "I need help savin' one of God's creatures."

She nodded at Melvin who stood but kept his head down. The other children stared, each looking like Melvin, except larger or smaller, height wise, which wasn't big even then. Melvin was second to the tallest.

The largest boy reminded J.J. of the orangutan at the zoo, ready to spit out anger to protect his territory, the same brother who was just another threat to Melvin at school.

"Melvin," his mother called, closing the catalog, holding it to her breast with slender hands as if it were precious. "Offer your guest something to eat."

Melvin made his way to the cupboard, taking out a lonely box of Krispy saltines.

"I'm full as a tick," J.J. lied. "My lunch would have fed three small foreign countries."

Melvin thrust a cracker at J.J. who was a box-of-crackers hungry. Embarrassed, he accepted it so they could get on with snake business.

Mrs. Beasley, Melvin's mother, had obviously been *raised proper*.

"We're on a shopping *twip*," whispered one of the girls.

"You're ordering stuff?" J.J. asked.

"It's a *dweam twip*," another little girl said. 'We just *wiss* for *fings*. I just *wissed* for some *unnerwear wiff Voody Voodpecker* on it. I don't got no *unnerwear weally*."

The orangutan-brother raised his head, his right hand held in the air, as if to strike her. J.J. made mental fists in his head just in case. He couldn't tolerate anyone hitting a little child like that.

J.J. motioned for Melvin to follow him, tipping a pretend hat to Mrs. Beasley.

"You probably see snakes all the time," J.J. explained as he and Melvin left the dark room, walking out into the last of the daylight sun.

"I live in town. It's not that I'm afraid, Melvin. I just knew you were the right man for the job. I might end up choking it too hard or something."

Breaking the cracker in half, he gave the lion's share to Melvin who licked it, taking teeny bites, finally washing the salt off his hand with his tongue, leaving a little pink spot in the grime.

J.J. opened a package of LifeSavers, eating a red one, his favorite, handing the rest to Melvin. As an afterthought he felt guilty not having handed Melvin the whole pack. It was too late to give him the already-wet red one.

"To thank you," he said anyway, "if the snake's not already squashed."

When they reached the curvy lake road, the snake was unbloodied, still coiled in a spot of sunshine, looking as if it were hiding a treasure.

Melvin grabbed it by the head with one hand, lifting, wrapping it around his arm. A tiny little muscle bulged on Melvin's arm – really tiny.

Standing there held up by Melvin, the snake looked extra heavy. Maybe it really was as big as half a dollar or maybe even a silver dollar.

If the story were retold, J.J. would have to refer to it as a boa constrictor – escaped from a zoo probably.

Melvin freed his arm from the coils with little concern when he reached the grass, flexing his little bulge of muscle.

Mr. Stripe slithered through his stemmy home out of their sight. To retell the story, J.J. would have to come up with a name more threatening than "Mr. Stripe." He would call it a threatening serpent.

Seconds later a car raced by.

"You saved its life!" J.J. shouted.

As expected, there was no response from Melvin. In wordless agreement, the boys just turned and started back to Melvin's house where he could join his brothers and sisters in their *dweem* shopping.

J.J. wondered if Melvin *dweem shopped*. What would he dream for? shirts? blue-jeans? socks? a real Halloween costume? Pork and Beans?

Melvin fingered the package of Life Savers reverently on the walk back.

J.J. watched his face, wondering if he were methodically figuring out how he would share them with the others. He secretly hoped Melvin's sweet little sister got a cherry Lifesaver and not one of the nasty pineapple or lime ones -- nothing against limes or pineapples in general. It was a personal choice.

He wished he could remember how many Lifesavers were in the multi-colored roll? Would some of the kids have to split one?

When they reached Melvin's yard, his father was home, standing by the door, arms crossed – watchful, angry perhaps.

He, too, was skin over bones; his lip had the same curl.

Melvin's head drooped when he saw his father, and a skinny arm reached out, pushing J.J. into the road.

"You're lucky," J.J. said sincerely. "You've got a nice mom, and your house is almost as big as a teepee. . .I wish I had brothers and sisters. And your backyard looks like a dime store painting."

9

"Melvin!" J.J. continued. "You're a real friend."

Melvin stopped, turning in disbelief, lifting his head briefly, the look on his face connecting with reality; briefly, but connecting.

"Melvin," J.J. began with embarrassment, "about Halloween. I knew you were Cream-of-Wheat-man. You shoulda' got the prize. The other kids were—well, just jealous."

J.J. kicked the ground, hoping his new friend had bought the story.

When he turned to look behind him during his journey back to the drug store apartment, Melvin and his father were nowhere in sight.

In Trouble Again

J.J. kicked the ground, wondering if Melvin believed he could have won the Halloween costume contest.

It was awful his brothers and sisters had to stay quiet and indoors while they lived where they could laugh without bothering their neighbors and run barefoot without worrying about nails.

The air was sweeter than uptown over the drug store on the square where cars were starting, poofing up smells of wasted gasoline and burning rubber, not to mention the occasional horse.

Horses dumped on the brick streets with the greatest of ease, and their riders didn't pay any mind. How could anyone live in town and get used to the smell of horse crap? Why should he have to?

As J.J. continued to trudge toward town, he hoped by the time he got home his grandma would be off work. If not, he'd know there was some kind of banquet going on in the back room of the hotel, and he'd have to go there for dinner. That meant entertaining the customers, spinning on a bar stool, telling tall tales for the guests, mostly traveling salesmen with little money who were willing to stay at a run-down hotel in order to save a couple of dollars.

Having been in the hotel with strangers so often, J.J. was half afraid to look at the wanted posters in the post office. He imagined flipping through them saying, "There's Ben who likes heavy cream in his coffee. That's Merlin who always orders the pork chop dinner. That's Bart who never thought to mention he was a serial killer."

J.J. was getting closer to town as he walked. He had reached the curve where he could see the town ahead, the tower of the city courthouse and the old clock. The enormous hands on the clock had to work harder at saying noon than they did 6:30. The big hand made such an effort at 11:55, J.J. wanted to climb up the front of the courthouse and push the hour hand the rest of the way up to the 12. It then flopped right on to12:05 as it donged, making up for lost time.

J.J. would like to have hung around the statues in front of the courthouse, but the sheriff was particular about those statues, saying if he let J.J. play there, every old drunk in town would think they could hang around the statues and sneak behind them for a quick, easy bathroom break. Bathroom break was one of them *careful words* the sheriff used, trying to set a good example.

And the sheriff didn't chew either. J.J. never had to stand out of the line of fire for fear of being splattered with tobacco cud like he did with some of the other men in town who hung around the courthouse.

The courthouse, even in a small town, was busy. J.J. frequently went inside and walked around, wondering if some day he'd be one of the lawyers with a leather briefcase or maybe a judge with a black robe.

The sheriff kept warning him he was going to get a closer look at the judge.

Funny, he never wondered if he would ever become one of the old men who went down into the basement to play cards. That was probably because most of the time he spent at the courthouse, he sat outside the courtroom door and listened. The sheriff said his gift of gab was starting to sound like those *gall darn* attorneys.

J.J. did have fantasies about the days cowboy outlaw Jesse James was said to have visited the town to see his girlfriend. In those days the jail was where the lumber yard stood now, right across from First Christian Church. Jesse had been dead many long years, long before Grandma was born, but Grandma held him up as a local hero like many did in the town. He was a legend. Grandma used to mention him sometimes and say, "Poor little Jesse. They killed his mama."

She never did mention the Younger brothers, also outlaws, even though their daddy had been mayor a hundred years ago, or so the city courthouse gossip said.

No place else in town smelled quite like the courthouse-- pine cleaner, polish and wax. Keeping the courthouse clean was not so different from life, J.J. thought. The more water that was used to clean the dirt away, the more feet that came in, mixing dust with the water, making mud. The *wet floor* sign just had to move from one spot to another.

Before J.J. got too tall, he had often stood under the round table in the foyer and studied the gum stuck to the bottom, hundreds, maybe thousands, of pieces in all shades of gray and pink, plus an occasional green or purple.

Some of the pieces were new enough there was a hint of Spearmint, Juicy Fruit and Doublemint smell under the table, depending on where he stood, and the sweetsie scent of bubble gum. Sometimes it was possible to even get a sniff of Teaberry gum, which came in the white and pink pack. There was a little flower on the package. Anyway, it looked like a flower. Black, of course, was licorice, Black Jack.

He sometimes poked and picked at the gooey mass, determining what was old and new – until Grandma saw him and scolded.

It was strange how she was concerned about "someone else's slobber" on the old gum; yet, she thought nothing of stopping on the sidewalk in plain sight of the whole world to lick her handkerchief and

J.J. grinned, showing as many teeth as possible. "I'll do better next time. I'll plan ahead and take a pillow and a cane so I can see over the steering wheel and reach the gas pedal."

"THERE WON'T BE A NEXT TIME!" the sheriff replied, rather hotly J.J. thought.

The sheriff slapped on his hat as if he were going to leave, but he pointed at J.J. "Why've you been at the lake? You aren't even carrying a fishing pole. Do you just roam all over the place?"

"Pretty much," J.J. said.

"And getting home after dark?" the sheriff shouted. "A car load of hooligans from the woods could pick you up and tear you apart. Do you ever think about that? You do realize a whole family was just killed across the state line?"

"No, Sir. I know this town is in the hands of our great sheriff. I salute every time I see your picture."

The sheriff pulled open the door to the hallway.

"How did you ever turn the car around when you decided to come home?" he questioned.

"Oh, I didn't," J.J. said. "There was a stranger there hitchhiking, and I asked if he would turn it around for me, and then he asked if he could drive me home. I said sure. He said he'd never driven a car before, but he did a darned good job I thought."

The sheriff's whole head turned a brilliant devil red, almost like in a cartoon. "So if he had murdered you and stolen the car, I didn't even have transportation to answer the call?" he shouted.

"But he didn't," J. J. said. "God watches out for children."

"And fools!" were the sheriff's parting words.

"You can't go without eating something!" Grandma Polly called after him. "At least take a piece of cake."

The sheriff had already reached the bottom of the stairs, having made use of his long legs to skip over a few.

"My wife and kids are waiting dinner on me – again!" he said. "It's goulash night —the first night."

The downstairs door slammed.

"What do you make of that, J.J.?" Grandma Polly asked, her lips trembling. "Do I have to follow you around? Take away your freedom?"

J.J. shrugged, making a spot in the chair where he could snuggle in deep, smelling and hearing the gurgling pan of boiling water heating up the hot dogs. He put his chin on the table and watched his fingers move around the fork and spoon.

He didn't answer.

There was no answer.

He ran with the wind, his arms reaching out.

He stomped in the rain, getting as wet as possible.

He rolled in the snow, sometimes almost sliding into the highway traffic.

When the weather was hot, he made shelters out of leafy branches at the lake and fishing gear out of sticks and safety pins

And, as he listened to the train whistle not so far away, he dreamed about catching a ride on a boxcar.

"What did the sheriff mean by 'the first night?'" J.J. asked.

"They'll probably eat goulash all week," Grandma answered but with a huff in her voice.

"The first night is the best. The vegetables still have a little life to them, and the meat won't have piddled down into flakes. She's probably using the pot roast left from Sunday dinner and added an onion to change the taste a little. She'll probably add a little something different each night, a tomato or some macaroni, maybe some chili powder."

J.J. halfway listened.

Grandma could help his restlessness and rebellion a lot, he thought, if she'd tell him who he was. He could accept the idea that he was an orphan, but she kept it all a secret, even his name.

Planting the Seed

Bobby Heath, the biggest boy in the seventh grade, stood at the edge of the playground, a crowd of other boys behind him.

J.J. surmised Bobby was looking for him. Well, Bobby couldn't prove J.J. had taken the pocket knife which Bobby had stolen from Paul.

J.J. had returned the knife to Paul, which seemed like a good thing to do. But Paul probably wouldn't tell Bobby he had his knife back, because Bobby would steal it again. Therefore, J.J. calculated, as far as Bobby knew, the knife was still missing, and no one but J.J. was swift and talented enough to take it from him without his knowing.

"Well, maybe this is good," J.J. said to himself.

The one piece of advice his uncle had ever given him about fighting was to beat the biggest guy, and then it wouldn't be necessary to take the others. He had proved his uncle wrong many times over, but it was still the only advice he had.

Ted and Ollie stood directly behind Bobby, and Adam and Todd to one side. Charles and Max were in the crowd somewhere probably, and all kinds of other feet J.J. didn't recognize.

Two sockless, dirty feet were crushing the heels of a pair of worn penniless loafers, and the shoestrings in the pair next to those were ragged, matching the tennis shoes themselves. One pair of scarred white bucks barely peeked through, way behind the others, Dave's probably, as his father was rich, and he wouldn't really fight. He would just be in the crowd so he could claim he was there and got in a couple licks.

Everyone would remember he was there, too, because only white bucks had orange soles.

"You boys have a problem?" J. J. asked politely, taking his eyes off the shoes after estimating the size of the kid posse, staring Bobby right in the eye.

During the contemplation, or time to do the math, he had made fists but let his arms hang at his sides, ready to defend himself but not start anything. In the principal's office, guilty came down to whoever threw the first punch.

He liked looking at the shoes first instead of the array of jelly-smeared cheeks and snot noses. Fourteen feet would mean *only seven* actual enemies.

"Now don't you look so innocent," Bobby said, making a fist as well. "Give us our money back."

Oh, so this wasn't about Paul's knife.

This apparently had to do not just with Bobby but with all of them.

"What for?" J.J. asked, not backing down. "You all got your chew."

He turned a full circle, checking out three sixth-grade girls who passed, looking back at him. It was always difficult to tell if they were flirting or just laughing at him. His ego preferred to think they were flirting.

They giggled. One turned to look over her shoulder and was almost run down by a boy dribbling a basketball across the schoolyard without watching where he was going.

"We all had to empty our pockets in the hall," Bobby said in exasperation. "This is the first seventh-grade shakedown in the entire history of the school! We're in trouble – almost all of us. I can't have allowance for a month. Danny can't go to the Dairy Queen all summer.

Ernie can't sit down without a pillow. And Gene's dad wants to know why you weren't caught with any tobacco yourself."

Bobby crossed his arms, waiting for an answer.

"Yeah, what he said," came from the crowd. "You lied. We got a bad deal. I still feel sick."

As brave as they all sounded, Bobby was always the spokesperson, and why not? It was rumored the high school coach planned to recruit him for varsity football when he reached eighth grade.

J.J. shook his head in disbelief, shooing them away. "You've got to be kidding," he said. "The stuff's nasty! I wouldn't be caught dead with chewing tobacco in my mouth. It stains your teeth."

"You didn't say that when you sold it to us," Bobby accused, although he was backing up, waving his arms forward to urge the others to chip in and say something.

"No," J.J. replied solemnly.

"I said, 'Do you want to buy some chewing tobacco?' and all of you stuck your hands out with money in your fists. There was no sales pitch needed or given. You were all dying to be first, afraid I would run out before you got your share, asking if I would be able to get more. I merely supplied the demands of the consumers."

The boys eased off.

He was right.

J.J. tipped his pretend hat and walked away, not looking back. After he had taken what he considered enough steps, he took something out of his pocket, holding it in front of him, cupped in his hand, so no one could peek. He kept walking. After a few minutes of hearing whispers behind him, he realized he was being followed, so his plan was working.

He stopped, and without turning around asked, "Do you boys want something?"

There was some hemming and hawing. "We wonder what you're looking at," Bobby said.

"No, you don't," J.J. said, starting to walk again. "It's something I don't want to sell, and if you see it, you'll want it, and if you buy it and get in trouble, you'll be mad at me. I don't want you to be mad at me anymore. I just want to be one of the boys."

"We promise we won't try and buy it," Bobby said. "We just want to know what it is. Let us look."

"Wellll," J.J. said. "I've already told the sixth-grade boys about this, and I think they're pretty interested. I don't want to cheat them out of what I promised."

"J.J.!"

He faced the lot of them, wondering how soon the school bell would ring. Perhaps he should wait until noon to share. He didn't want to rush this; it was too good to ruin because there wasn't enough time their mothers hadn't received a phone call at home, the event may as well have never taken place.

But now, there it was! His name – at least his last name and his first initials, right there on the envelope with one of Virginia's –or one of the other girls' – dragonfly, wingless exclamation marks. He had RE-ALLY been invited.

"You don't think we should really go to this?" Adam asked. "Do you? Formal sounds like we're supposed to wear dresses or something. I think the girls are dreaming things up to feel like big stuff."

Ollie took his seat in the classroom, shaking his head, leaning back, a man of authority. "Ever since the girls got brassieres, they haven't been no fun anymore. They're just not the same," he said.

"I've enjoyed the brassieres," Gene said, laughing. "I've liked looking at them – well, not actually *at* them –but you can tell they're there. Some of them look like ice cream cones. *Ja* ever notice that?"

"Personally, I like snapping them," Danny said.

J.J. was just embarrassed.

"Sure, we'll go," he said, sliding into his seat, finally answering Adam's question. "I was just deciding if I should wear my gray suit or my black one or maybe I should buy one of them pinstriped ones like attorneys wear. The sheriff is counting on my becoming an attorney, you know. He thinks I have the gift."

He stuck his invitation down the front of his shirt as if there were a pocket on the inside like in a suit. "I haven't had a suit like that for goin' on three years," he said.

As long as he was the last one to stand up at lunch time, no one would see the invitation fall out, giving away he did not have an inside pocket.

"J.J., you haven't got any suit," Danny said. "You're just saying that. No one who doesn't go to church doesn't have a suit, and my mother said you never saw the inside of a church in your whole life, and neither has your old granny."

"Have so," J.J. said, jumping out of his desk, prancing up to his nemesis, staring him straight in the eyes and then realizing the invitation had fallen out of his shirt onto the floor.

Hoping no one noticed, J.J. continued his defense. "Uncle Fred and I painted the Episcopal preacher's office just last summer, and that's right in the middle of a church – and I've got a suit.

"You think my grandmother hasn't taught me anything? I once went to one of those big dinners where everyone gets a whole set of forks to eat with. There's even a little teeny one for picking your teeth. They used those extra big tables, because the forks took up so much room. I had my own little knife just for butter and a saucer just for the roll.

"The pig with the apple in its mouth was so big, it took six grown men to carry it from the kitchen. It smelled like a huge pork chop. I didn't even spill my soup, not that there was hardly a place to set food anyways with all those forks and things. We paid lots of money to eat that night, and the maids brought the food out one plate at a time. The president was there – or would have been if he'd known about it. I sat across from a movie star, and he got gravy on his tie. It was red."

The faster he talked, the bigger J.J.'s eyes grew.

"What kind of gravy is red?" Max asked.

'No kind," J.J. said solemnly. "The tie was red, and the gravy was gray-brown. It was pig gravy."

"Who was the movie star?"

"Tab Hunter."

"A TV man held a microphone right over the top of the gravy spot so no one could see it, but I'd seen him do it. When we finished eating, the maids came and got the dishes and put them on a little elevator."

Ollie leaned to the side so he could talk to J.J. from his seat. "You didn't spill any soup, because you drank out of the bowl," he said.

"There's nothing wrong with dreaming big," J.J. said, glad he'd seen enough tables set at the hotel for special dinners that he knew about all the forks and the little butter knife. He'd seen the little elevator for the dishes in a *Three Stooges* movie.

Plans Expand

J.J. was still thinking about the dance when lunchtime came. He sat in the classroom, holding in his grubby hand, half a baloney sandwich stuck together with Miracle Whip. Most of the class had paid for their lunch.

They were eating what J.J. called "dog food," but secretly he wished he could eat in the cafeteria. There was never enough money to do that.

He could have worked for his meals, but Grandma Polly didn't want people to think they were poor. He could smell corn from where he sat on the second floor of the old brick school. Corn always smelled good, even raw. But added butter created a heavenly cologne. The smell of butterey kernels kept him from being able to concentrate, much like seeing a cute girl.

He sniffed extra hard, wondering if the cooks had made cobbler. They made a lot of cobblers.

People donated fruit to the cafeteria when it was in season. Grandma Polly knew the cafeteria cooks, and they called her when a load of fruit came in, baskets and baskets. They asked her to come peel, and she did, working it around her other duties. Before he was old enough to go to school, J.J. went with her and could eat all the peels he wanted.

During hunting season, there was plenty of venison. He loved the wild peppery smell.. One time lunch was free for everyone since the meat had been donated. The cooks even made dressing.

Grandma Polly didn't seem to know any generous hunters, and she wouldn't have taken free meat even if she did.

One time though, she gave him a deer steak at the hotel and told him she thought it tasted a bit "gamey." It was hard to know if it was gamey or not. There didn't seem to be a cow season when there were cow steaks to donate to the school, and Grandma had never given him a cow steak at the hotel. For her to have done that, someone would have to walk away and leave their steak on the plate after paying for it. That would have taken a miracle.

He had nothing to compare "gamey" with. He considered that "gamey" might mean the meat tasted a little bit like feet smell.

He sniffed again, letting the morning daydream by, just thinking about food – liver and onions? corn with liver and onions.

J.J. took one last long sniff — spice cake. The ladies had baked spice cake. Who could he ask for their spice cake without sounding needy? Perhaps if he caught up with Virginia in time. He could apologize for accidentally hurting her feelings that morning and could compliment her on staying so lovely by not eating desserts. It was worth a try if the timing worked out.

A few others with cold lunches had swallowed everything whole and gone out to play. Chubby Anita sat in the back of the room chew-ing on a tuna fish sandwich, quiet as usual. The few times she did go out on the playground, she stood around uncomfortably as if she didn't know what she was supposed to do.

Melvin was bent over his food as if it were going to get away. It was difficult to see what he was eating. Whatever it was, it had arrived wrapped in newspaper, and Melvin kept the paper covering his lips, secret like, no crumbs hitting the floor for the ants later.

"Beats me how you do it, Melvin," J.J. said, carefully edging his Butterfinger candy bar towards Melvin's elbow.

"This is for your dessert," he whispered, hoping Anita wouldn't hear him being thoughtful.

"You sit in class every day and do absolutely nothing, Melvin," J.J. continued. "And every year I expect we'll lose you to the class behind us, and then the first day of school comes, and there you are. Somebody plops you down next to me because we are the scrawniest kids in the class, except I'm built like a bulldog, and you're more like a Chihuahua."

He noticed Melvin's unopened party invitation lying on the desk, amazed but pleased the girls had remembered Melvin.

"Why you've got it made, Melvin. This school accepts you like you are. The teachers had a meeting years ago and decided it was OK for you to just ride along with the rest of the class. I doubt if we'd know how to act without you in the class."

Anita listened intently to the nostalgic sound in J.J.'s voice. There was no sarcasm. It was as if J.J. were just trying to help Melvin feel like somebody important.

"You know what would happen to me if I didn't answer the teacher or I didn't do my work?" J.J. continued. "I'd catch it. I sure would. I'd have to go to the principal's office and sit through a heck of a lecture, but not you. It took me a long time, Melvin, to figure out how to do just enough work to pass without doing more than I have to. It's a science.

But you have even a better scheme worked out. To make it work, you never say *anything*. I'd about die if I couldn't say anything."

"Amen," Anita whispered in the back of the room.

J.J. turned to give her a "look."

"You sayin' grace back there, Anita?" he asked.

Melvin shrunk, and J.J. thought of a turtle he'd had once which drew in its arms and legs when he touched it. Melvin's head had the same shape, and he had that funny lip like turtles in cartoons. If anyone noticed him, which they rarely did, he seemed to pull in his arms and legs, the big difference being that turtles peed when they were picked up, and probably – Melvin never got picked up.

As J.J. dreamed out loud to the other two slow eaters, a teacher peeked in. "You kids finish up and get some fresh air before the bell rings and lunch is over," she said. "You've been sitting in here long enough. The air is stale."

She pinched her nose.

J.J. and Anita moved toward the door, but Melvin rolled up in a ball at his desk like a sow bug. Rolling up was more difficult for him this year, because the school had abandoned the old-fashioned desks with unnecessary inkwells and had gone to chairs with a place to write attached and a hole underneath for books and supplies. The supply hole became a conversation piece when someone put a carton of milk in it and let it sour, but that didn't happen every day.

J.J. liked the new type chair-desks, because each was separate from the other, so it was possible to scoot around when a teacher wasn't looking and bang into others. He wasn't the only one to have discovered this, so there were several chair wars. The important thing was to control the desk by holding on to the front to protect the fingers from getting smashed between chairs.

"Anita," J. J. said as they started toward the playground, "save a dance for me. I plan to ask every girl in the whole class for a dance. Save me a dance now, Anita, and save one for Melvin."

He turned on his heel, running back to the classroom.

"How about that, Melvin? We'll go together, the two of us! We'll have the time of our lives and borrow some Aqua Velva aftershave from the man who lives across the hall from me."

Melvin stirred slightly, becoming tinier in his desk if it were possible. He seemed to shrivel, skin stretched over bone, pushed into a pair of enormous overalls.

"I'm serious," J.J. said solemnly. "I'll go talk to your folks if you want, and we'll get them to let you go, and I'll find you a suit. You'll look like a million dollars. You won't be able to keep the women off you, Melvin, and the food will be great. Maybe they'll have one of those big cakes with candy flowers on it like the ones in the bakery window. They'll probably have strawberries and oranges floating in the Kool-Aid – or sherbet! Sometimes I've heard there's sherbet in the bowl! Maybe the bowl will be decorated with real diamonds!

"But we can't stick our fingers in the icing at this big event. We'll have to accept a piece of cake on a plate given to us by a beautiful woman like in the magazines. We'll bow and say, "Thank you, Mam." We'll have a ball."

Anita had followed J.J. back into the room as if incapable of walking to the playground alone. She always seemed to want to follow someone. Even though she was quiet, he knew she was there because she had an aggravating habit of smelling like soap and perfume.

"Anita! Remember to save a dance for me now, and save one for Melvin," he repeated.

"We could practice," she said shyly. "I have two friends, Marvin and Tim, and we could all practice."

"Do you realize," J.J. said with sheer disbelief, "that if Melvin and I were to be seen with Marvin and Timmy, we'd be known as one of the misfits? You SHOCK me, Anita."

"When you get time to listen," Anita replied, a little more boldly, "I'll tell you something you obviously don't know --You're already one of the misfits."

MAKING A SALE

When school let out, J.J. was surprised a crowd of boys were waiting for him under one of the trees.

"WHAT?" he said. "I've minded my own business all day."

"But," started Bobby, jabbing J.J. in the chest, "you were going to show us something at lunch, and you didn't come out on the playground till the bell rang. We want to see what you were looking at this morning."

"How do you know I didn't give it to the sixth graders?" J.J. asked.

"Because they were outside with us, and they said you hadn't said anything about nothin'."

"Well, OK, but this isn't anything I can sell. I got these special at the source where I get the cocktail wieners and artichoke hearts I sell to the ladies for parties, and there was only one deck."

"Cards?" Bobby groaned. "You just have a deck of cards? What are they? OLD MAID?"

J.J. shrugged and started to put the card box back into his pocket.

"Wait!" Bobby shouted. "What's that on the front of the box?"

"Just some ol' neck'ed lady, Bobby. Like I said, you fellows don't really want to get mixed up with these. Having two or three of these would be worse than being caught with chewing tobacco."

The oxygen around J.J. dissipated as the words "necked lady" perked up the ears of the other boys.

"OK," J.J. said with a sign. "I'll pass around one card, and you can all look at it."

"I'll be darned."

"Will you look at that."

"Cripes."

"Let me see it again."

"How much you want for this, J.J.?"

J.J. said nothing until all of the boys were staring at him.

"Thirty-five cents each," he said. "They're all different."

"That's highway robbery! someone shouted. "Fifteen more cents, and I could go to the show Saturday!"

J.J. shrugged, frantically dealing out cards and taking money, counting the coins and moving on to the next boy until all the cards were gone. The boys left smiling at one another, already trading.

"I love happy customers," J.J. thought, running to catch up with Melvin who was straggling along behind some of his brothers and sisters.

J.J. touched Melvin, gently, giving him a soft, playful little punch on the grubby elbow. Melvin put his hands deep into his overalls pockets and let his head droop so low that from the back, he seemed to have no head at all.

As they walked, J.J. talked and called out to every seventh-grade girl they passed. "Save me a dance now, and don't forget to save one for Melvin!"

Melvin's neck flushed scarlet, but he said nothing, just continued to push forward, continuing to listen –or at least he appeared to. He sneezed once and put his hands over his face as if he expected J.J. to hit him.

"I'm sorry I didn't think to save you a card with a neck'ed lady on it, Melvin," J.J. said apologetically. "Since we're best friends, I would have given it to you for nothing. I don't know what I was thinking."

They walked as far as the drug store together. J.J. didn't want to walk all the way to the lake; he wanted to take his card money upstairs and sneak most of it into Grandma Polly's food money jar.

Melvin would have just kept sauntering along toward home, but J.J. grabbed his arm.

"Melvin, I never asked anyone else this, but my grandmother and my uncle, but there's something that really bothers me."

Melvin lifted his eyes slightly, marveling, J.J. supposed, that anyone would ask his opinion about anything.

"My people have been calling me J.J. now for 13 years, and it drives me nuts not knowing what it stands for. I have thought of every *J* name I can. Bless it all, Melvin, I don't know what I would call myself if I were to give myself a name. Should I call myself John? Jim? Jake? Jeremiah? Jack-o-lantern?"

J.J. showed his teeth, trying to make a scary face.

He didn't expect an answer.

After all, Melvin never answered.

But he smiled just a little.

His head dropped quickly, but as he turned to walk away, J.J.'s straining ears picked up one word.

"Joe," Melvin said.

Convincing Grandma

Polly Baskin, smelling like cinnamon rolls and day-old, oniony sweat -- looked tired when she got home from the hotel. She made no complaint about being weary or having just come from work. She just took a pan from a lower shelf and started peeling potatoes.

It didn't disturb J.J. she smelled like sweat.

She talked about smells a lot. Every day before he left for school – if she were home—she would ask if he had "worshed."

Worshing to Grandma Polly meant washing his face and hands, standing at the sink, washing down as far as possible and up as far as possible and then washing possible. He had figured out young in life what she meant by "possible," but it all sounded ridiculous to him.

Early attempts to put soap and water on a dirty body just stirred up the stink, and there were no instructions for the back of the body. That made sense though. People didn't seem to comb the back of their hair either. Hair would be all smooth and fixed in the front and all flat in the back where it'd been slept on, not to mention that some kids went to school with "sleep" crusted in the corners of their eyes.

Grandma Polly apparently "worshed" every morning. She left the apartment smelling like Cashmere Bouquet bath powder and came home smelling like sweat – and cinnamon rolls, at the very least freshly baked bread. It was a nice combination, sweat and fresh bread.

Sometimes she bought what was called deodorant from a door-to-door saleswoman. It came in a little square bottle with a red label, and it looked like yellow water. Grandma only bought the deodorant because the sales lady limped, and Grandma said she, Grandma, was "giving somebody a job." She saved the deodorant for special occasions, but really, when she used it, over time she just smelled like sweat anyway.

"I don't know what we did before we had deodorant," Grandma Polly said one day right out of the blue. "I guess we all stunk, so we didn't think anything about it."

Grandma Polly never mentioned teeth much.

J.J. made sure his toothbrush was wet when he left for school, but it seemed he had had the same one forever, and he never ran out of toothpaste. Grandma Polly didn't have her own teeth. But the false teeth look went well with the baggy pink one-piece underwear she hung on the clothesline to dry. How did she get into that? There were no zippers or buttons. Apparently, she approached the garment through the neck, stepped into the leg holes, and then pulled the straps up over her arms. He didn't know. He didn't really care. But it was one garment that made J.J. glad he was a man.

Another routine he didn't envy was her having to roll her leg hose to just below the knee and fasten them with an elastic band called a garter. Her hose were heavier than young women wore, a grayish-pink color, and she wore them every day, rain or shine, work or Sunday. There appeared to be no "best pair of hose" for funerals and things. When she took them off when she got home from work, the garter left a deep circle on her leg that looked like a mayonnaise jar lid. He wondered why that didn't hurt, but she never complained.

It seemed to J.J. Grandma had worn the same house dresses his whole life, buttons down the front, one with a little lace on the collar for Sunday although it was true, they rarely, if ever, went to church.

He knew the dresses by heart. He'd see them in the morning all ironed and starched, smelling a little scorched sometimes by the iron; and then she'd come home with the dresses limp from sweating in the kitchen and leaning over steamy dishwater.

His favorite was lavender with the black and white flowers swirling around on it. She had often rocked him while wearing that dress when he was a little boy, and each year the flowers faded a little more. Some embroidered flowers that hadn't been there before appeared sometimes where she'd sewn a flower to cover up a worn spot.

With that thought, J.J. knew it was time to talk brass tacks with Grandma, not about smells and dresses, but about promises.

"What do you know about the Beasleys?" J.J. asked, following her around in the kitchen.

"Generations of poor," his grandmother replied, somewhat surprised at the question. "They don't take help either. The dad and most of the kids all have those malformed mouths, and I don't know what he does for a living, but they're clean as they can be living like they do, and that poor mother is worn out all the time, and why wouldn't she be with all those children – and always pregnant?"

"You know what pregnant means, don't you, J.J."?

"Yes, Mam."

Grandma bit her lip as she spoke, shaking her head in pity or disapproval; it was difficult to tell except when she was upset, she slammed things as she cooked and said more with the banging than with her words.

"I went to the tent church once, and they were all there in a row, not saying a word. Some of us got together some food at Christmas, and we took it out there by the lake shack. You wouldn't believe how cold that place gets. They stuff newspaper in the cracks. I don't know where they get the newspapers.

He – the father – didn't want to take the food, or so he said. He said to give it to someone who really needed it, and there were all those little faces, looking up with their big round eyes, like corpses."

J.J. watched and listened as she worked, but he took the lid from the sugar bowl, stirring the crystals with his fingers, then licking his pinkie and poking it into the bowl and immediately into his mouth for a taste.

The sugar stuck better to a wet finger. Years of experimenting had proved this.

The pinkie he had immersed looked so much shinier than his others that he was considering putting them all in, one at a time. As his right forefinger aimed at the sugar, Grandma Polly foiled the plan, raising her hand as if to smack him, but she didn't.

J.J. let his hand fall limp on the table.

"One of the ladies said we were all too busy to take the food any further, quick thinking on her part it was, and Mr. Beasley said he would be willing to take the food if she let him cut wood for her fireplace. He said they wouldn't touch the food until the work was done. So, she asked him to go home with her right then, although it was cold and snowing a little.

That night, Christmas Eve, he cut the wood. She only asked him to cut a little, but he cut up a whole big tree she'd had taken down in the fall. It's not that she needed the wood to heat her house. I don't think she even had a fireplace or a wood stove. If you ask me, the man has more pride than is good with those hungry kids."

J.J. crossed his arm, his face crinkling in doubt. "I don't think he could cut up a whole big tree in one night," he said. "And all that chopping would keep the neighbors up."

Grandma Polly kept peeling potatoes, just so, the peels getting longer and longer the more she talked. She could do that with apples, too, and she never wasted anything. She would fry the skins later or cook them with a little cheese.

"I wasn't there, mind you, so whole tree or not, it was a lot of wood," she finally replied. 'My friends don't make up stories like you do."

"Why'd you go to the tent church?" J.J. asked. "I knew someone who went there once. He said they passed around a bucket of drinking water, and there's just one ladle. He said there was a red bean floating on top of the water that fell out of someone's mouth. There weren't any other beans around – no potluck dinner or anything –so it had to have come from someone's mouth."

Not upset by his own story, J.J. picked up a slice of raw potato and bit into it, not really liking the taste, but hungry. The disappointing thing about a slice of raw potato is that it looked like a slice of apple but wasn't an apple.

Oleo was disappointing as well. It looked all creamy and wonderful like cake icing, but its looks couldn't fool the mind. It was like having a big wad of lard in his mouth.

Grandma Polly sighed, rolling bits of hamburger and onion into tiny balls as she continued. "I suppose some people think of us as poor, J.J. I don't know if I went to the tent church to see if there's any good I could do for those people, or if it's the only place I can go and look like upper crust."

She smiled at him over her shoulder. "But it never hurts to look in on what others believe and do some serious thinking about it. I do have to say no one looked at me as if to ask why I wasn't wearing a hat, and no one frowned and told me I was sitting in their pew. And I didn't get any *'looks'* for putting 15 cents in the offering plate. I'm not even sure they took an offering. I left 15 cents in a plate anyway. Fifteen cents will buy a loaf of bread, you know. Fifteen cents in the offering plate is like putting a whole loaf of bread in; it just doesn't take up as much room."

J.J. was cautious with his next comment. "You think Mr. Beasley has too much pride, but everybody in town talks about how you don't take tips at the hotel," he ventured. "If we're so poor, why don't you? You have a little kid to feed."

He tried hard to give her one of his *adorable* looks and reached for another piece of potato, but she slapped his hand for real this time.

"You don't look like a corpse, J.J. You look like one of the best fed kids in town, and maybe you are. I don't spare when it comes to feeding you. You've already got a belly on you. And most of the men who come into the hotel don't have extra money to give me just for pouring them a cup of coffee, *worshing* some dishes and listening to their stories – I kind of enjoy the stories. I'd be lonely without the stories. Those strangers at the hotel are like friends. All the people around here with money work in Springfield or own their own store, and the ones with stores go out and eat at the big highway restaurants. They want to have a menu that's not written in pencil."

"Daily special," J.J. joked, "special because no one ate it yesterday so it's cheaper today, and Lord knows we can't get away with serving it again tomorrow."

She shrugged, ignoring him. "Of course, the doctor comes in once in a while, and he ought to have money, but his receptionist tells me a lot of people can't pay. He's sure been good to us. He's never charged me once for your school shots. When I go in and ask what I owe, they always claim I already paid when I was in before. There's never a balance on my records. That's a big tip."

"He's sweet on you," J.J. said confidently. "Everyone in town says so."

Grandma Polly dropped the potatoes and meatballs into a skillet bubbling with hot lard, so J.J. got out of the way of the grease splatter, choosing to move to the living room where he could shout back and forth while hanging his legs over the back of the sofa.

"Maybe you ought to marry him," he yelled back.

His grandmother came out of the kitchen smiling, swatting him with a rolled-up newspaper.

J.J. ran away from her laughing, pointing at the newspaper. "Don't you tear up the best fly swatter in the house!" he shouted.

"I've got at least 15 years on the doctor, J.J. He's a very nice young man who's nice to an old woman."

J.J. wondered if it would be a good time to drop his bombshell. Should he ask her to solve his new problem or try and handle it on his own?

He waited a minute, giving her more time to talk more about the doctor if she wanted to. The doc was a good-looking man, and he smelled like spicy aftershave. He probably even *worshed* and put Brylcreem on his hair. J.J. knew from the hotel T.V. all about fancy products.

"Grandma," he finally said, weighing his words, "the whole class is goin' to a dance, and I need a suit, one for me and one for Melvin Beasley."

He sat up again so he could face her straight on, dark earth-colored curls falling into his face.

"AND Melvin Beasley?" she exclaimed, grinning. "Are you going to wear it at the same time or take turns?"

She sat down slowly as she spoke, easing into the rocker, trusting the meatballs wouldn't burn. J.J. figured she knew what the meatballs were doing depending on how they smelled.

"Melvin Beasley," she repeated before pushing her way out of the chair again almost instantly, heading toward the hot skillet. "My boy is going to a dance, and he's going with Melvin Beasley?"

"I promised him," J.J. said. "I said we'd be the best-looking men at the dance, and I told him we would knock the women dead. We'd wear killer suits. I might even get a date, Grandma. Should I do that? Should I get a girl for me and one for Melvin and buy some flowers, or is that asking too much of money we don't have already?"

He was at her heels.

"Well, give me a chance to get my brains together," she scolded. "You need a suit. You're going to a dance, and you want to buy a suit for a Beasley boy? I couldn't be more surprised if you had come in and told me you were getting married."

J.J. grinned. "Well, if the dance goes off like it's supposed to," he said, "maybe I will get married."

He grabbed a cold green bean before Grandma turned on another gas flame and set a round cook pan over it. Cold green beans, even when hungry, were as disappointing as raw potato slices and oleo.

"Oh, hush, J.J. and stop fooling," Grandma Polly replied. "Of course, I'll get you a suit. It's probably time you had one anyway. We'll go down to Mr. Makin's store up the street and pay some a week at a time until it's paid up. In the meantime, you can wear it to the dance, but I'd appreciate it if you'd go to church with me once or twice, too, and get some wear out of it."

"Does that mean you'll be getting a new dress?" J.J. replied.

She stirred the canned green beans fast although they didn't need any stirring, stopping only to cut up a piece of cold fried bacon to add in and pouring in some of the grease from the meat and potatoes.

"It's a deal," J.J. said, "but going to church just to wear my suit out doesn't sound like a very good reason for going unless you get a new dress out of the bargain. And the kids at school claim you've never stepped inside a church."

He backed off, considering again. "How about Melvin?" he asked, his eyes pleading. He didn't want to push the issue, but he had promised.

Grandma played with her apron and looked out the kitchen window to the west although all she could see from where she stood was the funeral home and furniture store across the street.

"J.J., I do well to take care of one boy, and although I'd like to help the Beasley's – I would give them food and underwear if I had it to spare – I can't afford to buy their boy a suit. No one told them to have all those babies."

Her mouth was set tight. That would be the final answer.

"How about socks then?" J.J. asked, starting to set the table for good luck.

She nodded reluctantly. "Put me down for socks," she said, "and I'll get out one of your old shirts. I don't know where else to go after that. You've worn your clothes plum out."

J.J. kissed her on the cheek and grinned. "To show you I'm grateful, no cookies for a month. That's a promise. If you don't buy cookies, that will pay for the socks."

He pondered.

"No cookies for a week?"

"You have little enough as it is," she said. "I won't take away your cookies. Besides, you already paid me back by promising to wear the suit to church. I don't have to buy cookies, you know. They give me the old leftover ones from the hotel."

J.J. nodded, trapped. Maybe he could talk her into going back to the tent church. Maybe Melvin would be there, and she wouldn't need a new dress.

"Blue, I think," J.J. said. "My father always favored blue before the president sent him off to do that spy mission in communist territory, you know. He got killed, Ben. He begged to be buried in a blue coffin, and the communists wouldn't let him. No, Sir. They said it had to be red because he died in their territory. That's why when I'm grown up, I'm going over there to dig him up and bring him back here and put his bones in a blue coffin like he wanted."

"That's mighty human of you, J.J." Ben said, smiling as J.J. made his selection of canned meat on the shelves. "I don't believe you ever told me about your father. You must be very proud of him."

"Oh, yes" J.J. said, "and it's too bad what happened to my mother. Don't you think?" He eyed the candy jars with desire but had business to conduct and had to watch his pennies.

Ben turned, eyes wise, interest pouring out of them. "Your mother? Do you mean your grandmother? Did something happen to her?"

As he spoke, he took down several jars of cocktail wieners from a high shelf and rubbed away the dust.

"No, Ben, I'm talking about my real mother. Why I thought every-one knew. She was married to my father before she married that island prince. And then one day she died in a terrible accident. I think she was eaten by a snake, bless her soul. My grandmother has news clip-pings about it. Really big snake."

Ben nodded, playing along.

"Your mother was a princess then?"

JJ. nodded. "An island princess. If you look really close at the news-paper clippings in my grandma's scrapbook, you can see some of my baby pictures. My baby booties are made out of that kind of furry-fuzzy material that gives you the shivers."

"Velvet?" Ben suggested. "So, the island gets cold sometimes?"

J. J. nodded. "Velvet. They all rotted, but I still have a little tiny crown wrapped in party paper. I couldn't lay my hands on it immediately, but I think it's in the cedar chest."

Ben chuckled. "Well, J.J., if you believe those papers in the grocery store, your mother and mine were both royal. And Teddy Roosevelt will be walking in the door with Andrew Jackson any minute."

"Who are they?" J.J. replied.

Ben laughed, but not so loud as to hurt J.J.'s feelings.

"If you ever leave town, who's going to keep me cheered up?" he said. "Everyone else who comes in gripes about the prices although I have the least expensive liquor in the county. Or they come in mad at their wife or husband – or already drunk. Some are here waiting for me when I open the doors – drunk."

"So why do you sell liquor?" J.J. asked.

"I don't know. This was my dad's store. I don't know what else to do. I'm knowledgeable about drink although I don't drink myself. – But today, wealthy or not, I got to meet a prince, and I've got a john to clean and whiskey to unpack. How many jars of little wienies do you want, and why again do the women love these so much?"

"I sold my first party pack, weenies and artichoke hearts, to a judge's wife," J.J. said. "I pointed out that no one in town had had a party with this particular brand which just happened to be the one Mrs. Dwight Eisenhower uses at her parties. Then after that I told the other women – in the strictest confidence – that this brand is the one the judge's wife uses to make her parties special. Sometimes the ladies are watching for me when I get to the door. I kind of keep track of when they're about ready for another party – or when I need money. Sometimes I have to plant the idea in their heads that it's time for another party."

J.J. sighed. "And sometimes I resort to my looks. I'm short, and I have curly hair, so I give them my best angel expressions and always say *mam*. I try and pass for nine—and some refer to me as 'sweet little boy'."

J.J. exhibited for his big friend an example of his *adorable* smile.

Ben just shook his head. "Don't try that on me. I just take straight cash for legal merchandise," he said. "You're on your own after that. I could try that on some of these old weasels who come in to buy whiskey, but I'd likely get my teeth punched out if I do," he added blandly.

J.J. laid a $5 bill on the counter and shook his head remorsefully, going over the story he had told about his dead parents. He took the sack of goods he had purchased, promising to be back as soon as he got another order.

"I've got to make enough money to buy a suit," he said.

"Have a big movie debut coming up?" Ben asked.

"No, Sir," J.J. said honestly. "I'm going to a real dance with cake and strawberries and pretty dresses, diamond punch bowls, the whole bit, right here in this very town. I think it will be the biggest party this town ever threw. The whole seventh grade is going."

He stood up straight, looking Ben right in the eyes. The truth felt good; somehow it didn't require as much memory or conscience as making things up.

"I'm glad to be able to help provide what you need," Ben said, heading toward the back room. "You just keep selling those weenies and artichoke hearts soaked in sauce, and you'll be able to buy a fine suit."

"But in time for the dance?" J.J. said, mostly to himself.

Clutching the bag of weenies and hearts, he headed out the back door, thinking it was time for him to plant the idea that the judge's wife needed to have another party, and she would serve these imported-from-France culinary delights. Then again, maybe he should just stick with the word *imported* and not mention France. The products had to have come from somewhere other than town.

SAVED BY A GIRL

The challenging thing about being a business man is "keeping track," and always being one step ahead of whoever is following. It was important to always take the lead and be confident, like never admitting to the sheriff there was such a thing as conscience.

The day started like any other Monday; the classroom didn't smell so much like puppies because several had *worshed* for church the day before. It was quieter than usual.

When Deputy O'Reilly filled up the doorway with his mass, all of the children looked up in surprise, shaking the day-dream bats out of their heads to stare.

"Mam'," the deputy said to Mrs. Franks, the teacher, "I'd like for the boys to step out into the hall, just the boys."

Faces flushed.

Some started to reach for their pockets before getting out of their desks.

"Come on, Men," J.J. said, getting up, motioning for everyone to follow. "He said he just wants us brutes. Let's go see how we can help. We're probably going to have to help pull dead bodies out of the river or something. There's probably been another attack of water moccasins down at the lake. Or maybe he just needs something heavy carried."

"And hold your hands up where I can see them!" the deputy demanded. "Don't touch your pockets! We'll take care of that in the hallway."

J. J. shook his head in wonder, mumbling, "Pockets again."

The girls looked on in question and amazement as did Mrs. Franks.

"Let's continue reading *Little Women*," Mrs. Franks said. "Anita, close the door please. Judy, you start reading where we left off."

The door closed, the mystery going with it.

"Empty your pockets," the deputy said. "Then pull them clean out and let me see the lint."

He watched as the boys oh so slowly pulled things out of their pockets, little knives for one thing, as everyone carried one, even the girls; no one knew when there would be a thread to cut or a dead lizard to poke at.

Pocket knives were just a utensil, a readiness for when someone said, "Help me open this box. Cut the string." They also came in handy if a fella wanted something to do. He could throw his knife at a tree and try and make it stick or as a last resort, clean his fingernails with the blade.

Coming from the boys' pockets was candy, some wrapped and some just linty; rocks of several varieties; odd-shaped pieces of trash rescued from the playground; sticks of gum; and broken pencils. There was one worse-for-wear snake skin.

Melvin's head was hanging down as always. He had nothing in his pockets. J.J. had three quarters, five pennies and half a moon pie, the sticky wrapping having already picked up any pocket debris, nothing that couldn't be wiped, licked or bitten off.

Some of the boys' heads were hanging even lower than Melvin's, and it seemed to take forever to know the real reason for the deputy's being at the school. Then it came to light -- playing cards with pictures of nude women on them.

Was one of the boys actually crying?

J.J.'s eyes searched each of their faces, realizing just as the fate of the other boys was in the hands of their parents, his fate was in their hands, not just the boys in his own seventh grade class but the boys from the "other" seventh grade class next door.

He quickly did the math. If there were 19 kids in each class and at least half of them were boys, he could be tarred and feathered by at least 19 boys total, and some of them had girlfriends – not to mention big brothers.

J.J. was doomed.

Then again, maybe not.

He didn't have any cards, so while the others were being punished, he might just have time to leave town if he didn't pack a bag. He could jump on an empty car at the railroad. He'd heard of people doing that. Shoot. He'd dreamed about it. Of course, sometimes they lost their legs or got cut up totally. He would probably have to join a circus with what was left of him. Maybe all that would be left was his head, and he'd have to roll everywhere.

Following 10 minutes which seemed like hours, the door to J.J.'s classroom opened unexpectedly, and Mrs. Franks walked out with Alyona Ivanov. By this time salty sweat was pouring down the faces of the boys as they waited to hear what their last day on earth would offer.

"I know this is unusual, Deputy, but one of my students has something to say in defense of her classmates, and there may be something to what she's saying," directed Mrs. Franks.

"I'd appreciate it if you would hear her out and then ask the boys to give you the cards. I believe we all know where they came from. The boys' money should be returned to them.

"As for punishment, letting their parents know is punishment enough. I'm sure most of them would consider being –expelled – forced to go home – more of a treat than a punishment. And I would rather have them in class learning something than sitting at home watching *Zorro*."

Alyona had only been with the class since the beginning of seventh grade. She was beyond intelligent and lived with her parents and grand-mother in a nice apartment. Her grandmother spoke only Russian.

Alyona's English diction was perfect; her questions in class always to the point. Each time she raised her hand, she began by saying, "I have two questions," and she always did. She had an easy laugh, and her dark chocolate brown eyes sparkled somewhere behind the frames of her far-too-big glasses as if she had just heard something funny.

She enjoyed being a ballerina; that was a career goal actually, even with her math and science skills. She had spent hours telling Chubby Anita the difference between just taking ballet lessons and actually be-ing a real ballerina.

The class was still *circling* her somewhat, not quite sure what to think of a dark-complexioned girl with straight, short black hair and no make-up.

The no make-up was noticeable because the other girls in the class, the ones who had been born in the United States, were already experi-menting with bottles of creamy *base* makeup on their skin and tubes and tubes of lipstick. When recess ended, the students having returned to class, Mrs. Franks had to call for closed compacts which sent click, click, clicks across the room.

"Sir," Alyona began, standing straight and looking directly at the deputy. "One of the boys," she said, giving Ollie a knowing wink, showed me his card on the way home from school last Friday. I thought perhaps the distribution of the cards would have somewhat of a volcanic reaction, so I asked to borrow it to take home to my father to get his take on it if anything should happen. Obviously, the volcano has erupted, and something is happening."

She smiled, and J.J. thought she had the whitest teeth he'd ever seen in his life. She obviously really used her toothbrush.

By now, Alyona had the full attention of everyone in the hallway, most of all J.J., who would never have expected the elementary school's one intellectual would take on his case. Yes, that's what she was doing, standing there like a lawyer, a lawyer with remarkably white teeth.

"My father is a Russian mathematician," she continued. "He's in this country ..." She stopped to laugh, "building a better mousetrap or something. I don't really know. but he is also highly skilled and studied in the world of art, a consultant at a university.

" I showed him the cards, Sir, and he pointed out that the playing cards the boys bought were not photographs but typical pin-up art from the 1940's and even before. One might also note, Sir, that although the women are without clothing, there is nothing showing if you understand my meaning. Their limbs are so carefully placed against their person, they are giving away no secrets. The focal point of most of the drawings is a hat. Some of the hats are positively elegant.

"My father pointed out there are worse things to be seen in magazines sold in the drug stores – in plain sight. He pointed out particularly the actress Jane Russell on the very covers – not just on the inside pages -- of movie magazines with Marilyn Monroe coming in as a close second, regarding exposure. Need I go on? And, again, those are actual photographs."

"So, what's your point?" the deputy asked.

"The boys were *very stupid* to give up their money for something they can see on a drug store shelf without evening opening the cover of a magazine," Alyona stated with great dignity.

"The beauty of stupidity is that it's a punishment in itself. Their money's gone, and they could have been seeing something much bawdier, if that were their goal, while drinking a Coke. Granted the magazines would be more expensive and more easily discovered by their mothers unless they just sneaked a peek, which some of them may already do."

"And the young man who sold these cards?" the deputy asked. "You think you have that all figured out as well?"

Alyona blushed, trying hard not to look at J.J.

"Some of these young boys bought the cards because they liked looking at the bared arms and legs of these caricatures of real women. Others – I believe – realize that not all of us have equal opportunities for survival and amenities. Some of us may have to – come up with ways to make money to help out at home. We may not discuss these things on the playground, but we all know they exist. Some boys might sell vegetables out of their garden. Others – don't have a garden. They sell what they can find."

"How old are you again?" the deputy asked Alyona.

"Twelve, Sir. I'm younger than most by a few months. I've been tutored in a private school."

"Mrs. Franks?" the deputy continued.

"I would say no recess for a week, but that's just a punishment for me," the teacher replied.

"As I said, I recommend their giving the cards back to you, and the – perpetrator's -- returning their money. Then we notify all the parents. They do the rest."

J.J. wanted to say the perfect thing. He wanted to get back to talking about the dance. He didn't like being outed. It had never dawned on him that the boys not only bought his ideas for the excitement but to help him out.

What if the ladies who bought his weenies and artichoke hearts felt the same way? What if everyone saw him as the poor kid – worse off than even Melvin because Melvin had parents.

Without being asked, he handed the quarters and pennies he had to the deputy and returned to the classroom with the other boys. He hadn't given the deputy all the money, but no questions were asked. Perhaps that would be sorted out between the law and the parents later – and maybe they would just decide he was poor.

J.J.'s eye itched and watered at the thought. He reached up to scratch it before anyone noticed. He didn't want to be considered the poor kid. If he got beaten up after school, so be it. He would take his lumps. He probably deserved them.

Perhaps he should say thank you to Alyona, but he wasn't sure how. More than protecting J.J., she had probably made her case for Ollie who walked her home from school and showed her his card. He must have really trusted her. They were probably engaged or something.

Then again, maybe she wanted to save all the boys. She couldn't see a whole class suffer just because of J.J.

As for the boys, deep down he knew none of them bought the cards to help his cause. Logic said they just wanted the naked pictures. Alyona made that part up about their caring. Yes, surely she did.

She had a kind heart.

J.J. looked across the room gratefully.

Alyona just waved her hand and bent her head to one side as if saying, "It's OK. Think nothing of it."

She was beautiful.

If he ever got a chance to talk to her, and if he could do it without stuttering, he would thank her. And he would apologize for Grandma who, when she didn't feel well, said she suspected the Russians were spraying something in the air to make her sick.

Alyona was a Russian.

She would never do that.

She was too kind.

LAY-AWAY

Having made some sales to the women in town who wanted to have fancy parties, J.J. returned to P. K. Presley's, facing a suit head-on, standing on his toes so he could reach the slick-headed dummy which stood on a table.

He sighed. The dummy was wearing suspenders? Would Melvin need suspenders? What if he couldn't hold his pants up? He always wore overalls.

J.J. whistled, and the clerk said, "May I help you?"

"You can find me a chest of gold!" he said. "That's what you want for this suit? Fourteen dollars? Eisenhower didn't wear a $14 suit to his own wedding!"

"I'm sure he didn't," the sales girl answered with a smile.

J.J. felt she was looking at him with angel eyes.

"Can we lay it back or something?" J.J. asked. "Can we leave this on put-back?"

He banged on the counter, getting his thoughts together.

"You know what I mean."

He was angry at himself. The episode in the school hallway had eaten a big chip out of his ego.

"Put it on layaway?" the girl asked. "If you have $5, you can lay it away, but you'll have to keep putting money on it until it's paid for. Is it the right size?"

She straightened the dummy's suit, spiffing him up.

"I don't know," J.J. grumbled. "It's got two arm holes and the proper number of legs, but for $14 it ought to fit everybody in town. What's so special about this suit that it costs $14?"

The salesgirl flushed.

"Well, the back of the legs don't wrinkle when you sit down," she said, "I've been told."

"Anything else?" J.J. asked.

She eyed another customer, not sure J.J. was going to buy anything.

"Well, you don't have to wear the vest with the jacket or the jacket with the vest, so it's like having three outfits. The color goes with all colors of shirts and ties."

"Ties?" went through his mind. Things just get worse.

"Yes – Suzanne --," J.J. continued, reading her nametag, "but you'll have to leave that suit on the dummy until I can come up with the first money."

He bit his lip, knowing he would only make a few cents on the wieners because he had been paid in advance and wasn't likely to get much of a tip upon delivery. Businessmen had so many costs to cover.

"Do you get many calls for these?" he asked, feeling of the sleeve. "Are you likely to run out? Oh, shoot! Every boy in the seventh grade is going to need a suit. Course, I don't know how many people are going to have $14. No offense, Mam. Could you sort of push it behind the underwear or something, so he doesn't show up from the outside? I sure need this suit."

He got down on his knees, clasping his hands under his chin, wishing for the first time in his life he had brushed his teeth.

"I can't do that," Suzanne said with embarrassment, looking around as she motioned for him to get up off the floor. "But don't worry. This suit on the dummy is what we call a rack suit. In the back by the dressing rooms, we have 10 more, maybe 12. Five or six of them are probably this same size."

She lowered her voice. "We haven't sold one suit since I've worked here. A lot of people go to Springfield to buy their clothes or they go to the stores that have been in town forever. I'm a town girl, so I – don't shop here. I go to the regular stores in town. We buy from the locals."

She checked out the other possible customer again, seeming caught between selling the suit, even on layaway, or perhaps bagging a bigger sale.

"What do you sell a lot of?" JJ asked. "Being a salesman myself, that would be interesting to know."

He fingered the buttons of a shirt.

Maybe there was something he could buy and resell like the party foods.

"Around Christmas we sold a lot of red plastic flowers," Suzanne said, frowning and removing his hand from the shirt with disgust as she spoke.

OK. So, his fingernails were dirty.

"Coats were on sale in February, and about now it seems to be garden tools."

She pointed here and there.

J.J. nodded solemnly. "You may never have met him before his death, but my grandfather invented the hoe," he said.

"You wouldn't think it would take a lot of thought to invent something like that, but one day he was out in his fields – well, his men were actually doing the work. They were trying to break the soil with sticks, and Grandpa thought and thought, and finally he said they ought to get a little piece of tin off the outhouse roof and bend it. Well, you know the rest. He sold his idea and made a ton more money, and he spent it 'til it ran out. And the next person to go in the outhouse got rained on, because they ran clean out of tin pieces making hoes. They took the whole darned roof! Grandpa's in Hawaii now growing pineapples."

"You said he died," Suzanne responded. "You said I didn't know him before he died."

J.J. shrugged. "Well, he's never coming back to this town. He's dead to us. And you didn't know him."

J.J. had won himself a devoted audience. "Why did they call it a hoe?" she continued.

The conversation had become a test of his imagination.

J. J. scratched his head, pretending to have taken an interest in a package of women's hosiery.

"Grandpa kept saying, 'Hold it like this! Hold it like this!' but he had what they call lazy speech, and what people heard was, 'Hoe it like this! Hoe it like this!' It was actually called a '*hold*' for several years. Everything makes sense when you know the full story."

"Yeah," Suzanne said. "I think the workers weren't the only ones who got something from the outhouse. I think that's where your story came from."

She took the package of hose out of his hands and put it back on the pile on the table.

"Hold on," J.J. said. "I had more important plans for this, but here's $5. Put the suit back for me."

SAYING NO TO CRIME

When J.J. left the department store, he hitchhiked across town to his friend Gene's house, trying not to look too disappointed when Gene's mother opened the door.

"J.J." she said with surprise and disapproval, "What are you doing here? I told you I don't want my son with the likes of you. And that was before the tobacco incident, not to mention the whole card thing. He won't get an allowance again as long as I'm his mother. He just uses it to keep you in tobacco money. Standing with her hands on her hips, she filled up the doorway. She rubbed her hands on her apron as if she'd been doing dishes.

"Mr. Gage, Gene's dad, wanted to talk to me," J.J. said, wishing he were anywhere else in the world.

"I know very well who Gene's dad is! See you about what?" she demanded, not budging.

"I don't know," J.J. said honestly. He's a grown man, so I have to be polite and respect his request. I was surprised when he called. Maybe I broke something last time I was here. Maybe he owes me a dime. Maybe he wants to yell at me about the caricatures of the women."

"Caricatures?" Mrs. Gage shouted. "Caricatures?"

J.J. tried to see around her, wishing there were a hat in his hands to hold. The sheriff seemed to find words easier when he held his sheriff's hat in his hand.

"If you came for a dime, I'll give you one to get rid of you," Mrs. Gage said. "I'll give you a dollar for that matter," she said, reaching into her apron pocket and coming up with nothing.

"I could use a dollar, thank you, Mam, but I'd rather just see Mr. Gage and ask what he wanted so I can put that behind me. I don't want him thinking I was rude and didn't respond to his request. He can have a bit of a temper."

"Personally, I think you're up to something, and I don't want my son in on it, you understand?" she replied. "I'm going to go look for my sweet little Gene right now and make sure he's nowhere near you. You could have had him in jail over those photographs of yours! He's a good little boy. He goes to Sunday school."

"They weren't photographs, Mrs. Gage. They were caricatures, and nothing private was showing. They were mostly just arms and legs of pretty women. As I recall your little boy pushed other boys out of the way to buy – THREE!"

"He was only caught with one card!" she defended.

"No, Mam, he pushed three boys out of his way to get that one card. I witnessed it."

He signed, thankful Alyona was brilliant. Why didn't the explanation sound as smart as it did when she was doing the talking?

Laying his pride aside, J.J. said one more thing to get through the door. "Gene doesn't keep me in tobacco money. I don't smoke or chew. He – Gene –has a kind heart and wants to make sure I have food. We're poor, you know."

Mrs. Gage conceded on that note and motioned J.J. inside, no welcome on her face, pointing toward the TV room where Alan Gage lay in front of the TV, an empty shot glass in his hand. "You don't look hungry to me," she said quietly as she disappeared into the kitchen.

"I want to do some business," Alan Gage said when he saw J.J.

He lifted a bottle of whisky as if to offer J.J. a swig.

J.J. wondered what the glass was for; it didn't look as if he used it.

J.J. shook his head no, saying, "There are some things even I won't do."

He sat down without being asked, letting his head droop a little. "I figured you must have something bad in mind, having sent someone to threaten to knock my teeth out if I didn't show up. Lay it on me."

Gage turned off the TV, sat up, crossed his legs so one stinking stocking foot stuck out in front of him.

J.J. wrinkled his nose, thinking Gage's socks smelled like coffee that'd been in the pot for four days without being unplugged.

"I've got this job coming up soon, and I thought you could help," Gage said, hacking more than coughing, turning J.J.'s stomach as he spits into his handkerchief.

At least he had a handkerchief.

He could have just hacked into his hand and tossed it.

J.J. had seen men do that in the street.

J.J. turned the TV back on in spite of the fact he in no way wanted to pick a fight.

He knew staying alive meant having some show of power.

"You aren't stupid, Kid," Gage said, lighting a cigarette, plumping a nasty pillow and lying down again on the sofa.

He rearranged his stinky feet, the only scent in the room louder than his alcohol breath. "I'll only tell you what you need to know and no more."

As mean as she was to him, J.J. wondered how a mother as devoted as Mrs. Gage could end up with this bottom river scum.

"I'll leave before you tell me anything," J.J. said, sensing that *something* was rotten. "I shouldn't have come. I only came to keep my teeth."

"And your teeth aren't safe yet," Gage said, sitting up half way to take another swig out of the bottle. "And yes, if you hadn't shown up by tonight, I would have seen you were left in a pile with your mouth mashed. I sent you the message a week ago."

Gage jumped up suddenly, losing his balance, catching himself by grabbing the sofa and then wrinkling J.J.'s shirt collar with his right hand as he continued to clutch the bottle with his left. "This isn't for the sheriff's ears either!" he said.

Looking down at the enormous hairy hand which practically had him by the throat, J.J. tried to back off.

"It's not for my ears either," J.J. said.

"I don't want to hear any more."

He desperately wished he were bigger.

He envisioned his father, whoever he was, as a little person, dead on the street, too short to fight back.

"If you did tell, you'd have to prove it," Gage said. "We just need you to crawl through a certain pipe in a building and unlock it from the other side. That's all. You can beat it after that."

"Don't tell me who *we* is," J.J. replied. "Just let me leave now and find yourself another boy – your son maybe."

He turned his head just enough to bite Gage on the hand, and the grasp released along with a string of swear words; but in turn Gage smacked J.J. so hard he fell over backwards onto the floor.

J.J. put his hand up to his mouth to cope with the pain, wanting to cry but refusing.

"We could make the sheriff think you done it alone, J.J., whether you done it or not. Everyone in town knows you're always lookin' to make a buck. You haven't been in big trouble yet, but the world has its breath held, waiting for the day.

"The boys' home has a door with your name on it – or would that be a number. You're Number Thirteen, J.J., the bad luck boy. We could convince anyone you're even worse than that. We could turn you into 666, the devil himself, and it wouldn't take much convincing. You don't have money. You're gutsy, and most of the time you're draggin' around alone. In addition to that, you're always runnin' your mouth. You're a perfect set-up. You convict yourself with every lie you tell."

J.J. stayed on the floor where he felt safer. There was no place to fall from the floor. He was thinking to himself that his words weren't meant to be lies; they were meant to be stories.

"The sheriff knows me too well," J.J. said without much confidence. "He knows I play fair and wouldn't do anything to hurt anyone." He scooted toward the door on his bottom.

"Ten percent of everything we get, J.J. – Not bad. That means a couple thousand dollars for you alone."

Gage pretended to dangle a carrot in the air. "Tempting. Tempting. Tempting," he said, his cartoon yellow teeth glowing from his grin.

"Not everyone keeps their money in a bank."

"I won't help you," J.J. said.

He had the door open now and was talking loud enough to get Mrs. Gage's attention.

"I can do it without you," Gage said. "I just knew you needed money. I am trying to do you a favor."

He followed J.J. to the door.

J.J. shrugged. "If you want to do me a favor, leave me alone. You don't know me. You don't know me at all. You don't know who I have to be; you only know what you think I am."

Gage lit another cigarette and let it dangle in his lips while he pulled a roll of bills from his pocket, balancing his weight on the door. "Down payment," he said, extending the roll.

J.J. stuck his hands in his pockets, refusing the offer.

"I've got friends who won't think this is funny," Gage called after him. "You're wise and yet dumb, Kid. When I get turned down, I win anyway."

Standing out of reach, J.J. backed down the front steps, feeling braver as he got further away.

"Well, Mr. Tooth Decay got you," he said to Gage who was too far behind him now to hear. Somehow, those words helped J.J. feel he had indeed had the last word. He even smiled a little. Who would have believed Mr. Tooth Decay would sound like a good guy.

The air seemed colder as he walked home. There was no need to hitchhike. Hitchhiking was dangerous anyway, even in a small town. There was no way to know what kind of characters were driving through, maybe even carnival people.

He thought the bumps rising on his arms looked like a plucked chicken's skin as the breezes shivered over him. He remembered the snake in the road and was sorry he had mistrusted it. It could never be as evil as the man on whom J.J. had just turned his back.

Answers to Desperation

J.J. swung his feet in rhythm, banging them on the coffee table where he sat, staring out the window to the south at the falling rain and people running, although it wasn't cold.

He personally wouldn't have run, relishing the idea of poking along in a heavy rain on a spring day. If Grandma Baskin had seen him sitting on the coffee table, he would have been dead meat, at least yelled-at-meat, but he had to have some way to cope with the depression of not having enough money to pay for Melvin's suit in time for the dance. And no, getting up to no good with Alan Gage was not and would never be an option.

The dance was now just a week away, and J.J.'s suit was hanging in the closet. But even if Melvin's had been hanging next to it, there was still the question of shoes and a tie for Melvin—suspenders?.

There was the possibility of asking one of the other boys, but then he would have to admit he was trying to do something nice, and he wasn't sure that was best for his reputation.

J.J. thought he had the tie situation figured out actually. He and Melvin could enter the ballroom with their shirts open at the collar.

J.J. would carry his tie in his hand, and they could tell anyone one who asked – Well, HE could tell anyone who asked since Melvin didn't talk, that Melvin's was in his pocket. An open collar was a cool look, comfortable, like a successful singer in Las Vegas – according to the movies.

J.J. reached for the phone absently when it rang.

"Baskin residence," he said with affected speech. "Madam Baskin is out. This is the butler, Viceroy speaking. May I give the madam a message?"

"J.J.!" his grandmother's voice scolded.

His feet stopped banging instantly.

"Now, Grandma, at least I didn't say, 'Baskin's Pool Hall. Who in the hall do you want?' and I didn't say, 'Baskin's Funeral Parlor. You killem', we chillem'.'"

"The Methodists are having a rummage sale right this minute," she shouted back as if they were talking on two tin cans and a string in-stead of a telephone. "If you can get your layaway money back, they've got a suit you could get for Melvin. It's in pretty good shape and gray."

"I was hoping for a nice pinstripe," he began.

"J.J.!"

"And SHOES?" he screamed, suddenly realizing the importance of what she was saying. "Are there shoes?" He was already running to the door, pulling the phone cord with him.

"Shoes never sell," Grandma shouted. "They're likely trying to sell them for a few cents. But be careful to get some he can walk in. His feet are probably longer than your little stubby ones."

J.J. mumbled to himself all the way to the chain store, liking the idea of a quick solution, but disappointed he wasn't able to have Melvin "fitted." Maybe he could get Grandma to do that.

J.J. and Suzanne had planned for him to deliver Melvin to the store during a slow time, and she was going to stand with a tape measure and pins, making Melvin feel like Hollywood. Of course, she wouldn't do any actual cutting and sewing later. It would be all for show.

Suzanne was busy when J.J. first entered the store, so he tapped his foot until she finished with the other customer.

"What are you so impatient about?" she asked. "You'd think we had a date or somethin'."

He quit tapping his foot, looking seriously at her awe-inspiring blue eyes. Despite her overabundance of eye makeup, which a blind man could have seen a mile off, J.J. bit his lip, wishing he were older and taller. Her perfume would have overpowered the elephants at the zoo, a scent which brought to mind huge orange flowers shaped like loudspeakers, but he didn't care, fantasizing as he breathed in her essence, wondering if he were to ask her out --

"Forget it!" she said before he could dream any further. "I've seen that look plenty of times before. You're in the seventh grade for Pete's sake."

She shuddered. "I only date high school boys –well, perhaps I'd go out with an eighth grader if he was rich. Plus! What are you – four-foot-tall with cowboy boots on?"

"I can dream," he responded.

"Listen, I can't raise the $14. I need my money back."

He held out his hand impatiently.

"Well, crap," Suzanne said, setting down a stack of boxes. "If you'd bought that suit, I'd made a commission. Sure you can't buy it?"

"Wish I could. There's one I can afford at the rummage sale. Do you think you could pin and measure it like we planned? real official?"

He gave her his best adorable boy look.

"This stopped being official as soon as I lost my commission," Suzanne said. "The store will stick you two dollars for the inconvenience of having it put away. No one else could buy it while you had it put away you know. Some stores would keep all your money."

"Why don't you just take out a gun and put on a mask?" J.J. shouted, pointing his finger right in her face.

"You said you had a whole rack of those suits in the back!"

"Store policy, grubby little kid," she answered, pushing a stick of Spearmint gum in between her pretty poppy-colored lips. "Pay the whole $14 bucks plus tax and earn me a commission, or I take the suit out of layaway, and you leave two dollars for the store manager. You get back three dollars. I don't know why you didn't lay it away at the store where you got *your* suit. Apparently, your grandma gets to pay what she can when she can or people say. That's why townspeople buy from locals."

"But there's a limit," J.J. explained. "They wouldn't put two suits away for her when she only has one boy. There's also a limit, unfortunately, to kindness; and I'm independent."

He took out his wallet, looking at the half-dressed dummy which had once worn Melvin's Hollywood look.

"I'm sorry," J.J. said to the dummy. "My check hasn't come this month yet from my father who's a famous – I can't think of anything –but you're not real anyway, so you don't care. I don't lie to dummies, and I have been trying really hard not to lie to Melvin. I don't think he'd understand. He might never say another word to anyone, and he's only said one word to me."

Suzanne returned, pushing three dollars into J.J.'s hand. "Here you go," she said, adding, "What does the J.J. stand for? Jerky Joker?" She laughed at her own joke.

"Jeremiah James," J.J. said. "I was named for my father who was a famous defense attorney. He was killed in Cleveland while defending an innocent man. Tragic."

J.J. wiped away a fake tear as he put the three dollars into the wallet.

Suzanne put her hand over her mouth, still chewing her gum. "J.J., someday lightning is going to come right down out of the sky and rock you clean off your feet. I'd like to rent you some night and take you home with me."

His eyes lit up.

"You could sit up with my mother and make up stories about why I was late getting in, and I could go on to bed and get some sleep."

"Do I need to come back for any bargains you forgot to mention?" he asked, ignoring her prattle.

"I'm a businessman, you know; got to keep my eyes open." He surveyed the store, forgetting his hurry.

"The manager's got some Easter baskets back there he's selling for 50 cents," Suzanne shared. "They're 3-years old, but if you ironed the ribbons, probably no one would guess. The marshmallow bunnies and popcorn balls are made out of rock or feel like it."

She knocked on the counter to make her point.

"Are the toy bunnies still in the baskets?"

"Heaven's no!" Suzanne replied. "He's got those up there on a table. He's not so stupid he doesn't know he could still make a profit on those. They still look brand new. He just can't bear to throw out the baskets with the grass and stuff in them."

She looked around to make sure no one else was listening. "He should hire you to convince people those popcorn balls are weapons or something."

"I only sell quality," J.J. said. "I make a good profit, but I sell good stuff. If he weren't so cheap, he could put a little fresh candy in the baskets.

"Except for the chewing tobacco I sold recently, I've never had a complaint. The boys just didn't realize what a nasty thing they were wanting.

"Myself, I gave them a good lesson in life. You and I can talk about this some time when your boss comes up with a bulk price on the baskets and grass. You tell him to make me an offer, but no rock edibles."

Suzanne laughed. "He'll probably just steal your idea," she said. "I'll tell him you could go out in the town and sell things people won't come in here to buy! You'd be out there spinning yarns, telling those big stories, dodging lightening as it came down out of the sky trying to hit you. I expect a commission."

She kept laughing until he was out the door and then slipped the two dollars into her own pocket.

"That will teach him to work me out of a commission," she thought. "He's such a little sucker."

J.J. left for the Methodist church, not finding her humor amusing but finding the idea of getting hit by lightning fairly interesting, provided he lived through it.

It was an especially good daydream to have while it was raining. He could imagine his curls straightened out, standing up on top of his head. Maybe the lightning would send him through the air like a man shot out of a rocket, another fascinating concept. If his mom and dad were circus people and came back for him, that could be his job.

He supposed the church holding the rummage sale must be the one with the sign that said, "Freshly baked cakes." There was an old wheelbarrow and a lantern out on the church lawn to get people's attention, topped with a taped-on scribbled sign which said, "Some antiques."

In years to come J.J. might wonder why he didn't go immediately to buy the suit, but he stopped to look at shoes, not to mention the time he had burned up talking to Suzanne. As his grandmother had predicted, no one was paying attention to the shoes, and there were more shoes than he'd seen in his whole life, stacks and stacks, some good as new and others which should have been thrown away. Even they were good enough to wear as a hobo at Halloween.

He went through the piles carefully until he found the perfect pair, black and shiny dance shoes if there were ever dance shoes. He put them on the floor next to his own feet and saw they were longer. He signed, sticking them under his arm, feeling lucky. Just as he remembered the suit, he saw it – in a woman's hand.

"Wait! You can't have that!" he shouted, reaching out, trying to grab it. "I need that suit! I only came here to get it!"

The woman looked at him aghast. Mouths dropped open.

"For a child to try and take something away from a grown woman!" someone shrieked. "To have something like that come out of a child's mouth!" came another comment.

The voices were haunting.

"I can't believe how children are raised these days! We would never have acted like that when I was a child!"

"He needs a good whippin' he does."

"Ugly little brat."

"I'm sorry," J.J. said. "But I came here to get that for a friend who doesn't have a suit. There's a big dance coming up at school, and I thought..."

"Well, I'm thinking you're a disgusting child, and if I find out who your mother is, I'll give her a piece of mind for bringing you into the world," the woman said, folding the suit into her arms so he couldn't get to it.

"You should have been here sooner. The sale's been going on for two days, and they only started marking the prices down today to get rid of things. If you wanted the suit so bad, you could have been here yesterday."

"I just heard about it!" J.J. pleaded. "Listen, Lady, buy the suit and rent it to me. My friend just needs it for one night."

He got on his knees, and she walked around him, raising her eyebrows as she looked at others who were nearby. "Look what I'm having to put up with!"

"Boy, if you want to rent a suit, they've got places in Springfield where you can do that. I've got 25 orders for dolls I've got to start tonight. This one suit is going to make a lot of little suits."

"It's not fair! You can't use Melvin's suit to make doll clothes!" J.J. screamed.

"Melvin should have thought about that before he put his suit in the sale," the woman said, laying five dollars on the table with several other things.

With tears in his eyes J.J. handed his three dollars to a lady with kind eyes who was sitting behind an adding machine. The Methodist volunteer took the shoes from him gently, wrapping them in a wrinkled paper sack. "Keep the money, Sugar," she said. "You can have the shoes for free. They never sell anyway."

"These shoes sold," J.J. said through the tears, leaving his money on the counter.

The lady with the kind eyes looked around for support from her coworkers, still weighing who was right and wrong in the suit argument. She picked up one of the dollars, replacing it with three quarters and two dimes. "We're marking things down now," she said. "And they may not fit. There's no way to return them and get your money back."

Sadly, J.J. took the package and picked up his change. "Thank you, Mam," he said.

There were other people behind J.J. in the line to pay, but the cashier put her hand on his cheek and smiled.

"Not everyone understands what was happening here today," she told him, "But it doesn't matter. Jesus knows your heart, and that's what's important. I have a feeling you're a very good friend. Jesus is a good friend, too. You're not alone."

J.J. swallowed, just nodding.

With the bag stuffed under his arm and the money clutched in his fist, J.J. went back into the rain, watching up and down, walking around and around the town square, looking for the woman who had bought the suit, the cold, unfriendly woman of no understanding, the kind who won't listen. If only the suit had been picked up by someone like the kind woman behind the adding machine, the one who understood the purchase was important to a friendship.

His clothes were soaked, and he stopped by the apartment only to leave the package of shoes so they wouldn't ruin. Returning to the street again, he promised to beg her if he had to. He just had to find her.

At last, he saw her, still scowling as if she hated the world. How could someone with such a frown make dolls – unless they were voodoo dolls? She was carrying more packages and taking the last few bites of an ice cream cone, licking the sweetness from her lips with her ugly tongue. The ice cream had smeared just enough on her mustache to make J.J.'s stomach turn.

She stopped to look at some perfume in the drug store window.

J.J. followed her to Makin's store where he stood quietly behind a rack of raincoats while she talked about her charge accounts and theater tickets. She wasn't poor! Why was she buying the suit at a rummage sale? If she wanted to dress dolls, she could buy fabric remnants right there at Makin's store for almost nothing. Why Melvin's suit?

She spent 15 minutes looking through dresses, the ones that cost a fortune, some of them $30.

Mr. Makin rounded the corner. "You didn't bring your suit back, did you?" he asked with his voice while at the same time his eyes were asking, "Why are you lurking here by yourself? Where's your grandmother?"

"No, Sir, I was just admiring all the pretty things you've got in the store, thinking you sure are some salesman. I look up to you a lot, one businessman to another." J.J. saluted.

Mr. Makin just laughed, stopping to straighten the panties piled high on a table. J.J. put his hands behind his back, thinking he could never own a store if he had to do embarrassing things like that.

"Thank you, J.J.," Mr. Makin said.

"It must be nice to be rich," J.J. continued, following him around the store, hoping Mr. Makin would assume he was there only as one business man to another and not for any other reason.

Mr. Makin seemed to relax.

"I suppose so," came the reply, "and if I ever get a chance to find out, I'll tell you what it's like."

The mean lady was out of sight now, but she had not left the store. She had slipped into a dressing room to try on one of the dresses that cost a fortune. Her packages were lying on a chair by the dressing room door. There was only a curtain between the two of them.

J.J. could see her feet beneath the curtain, and her dress hit the floor, so he knew she must be standing in her underwear. She wouldn't be flying out to chase him any time soon.

It wasn't so unusual she had left her packages lying in sight as it was a small town, and in the stores which had been there forever, people felt safe. She had even left her purse lying out. J.J. didn't want anything but the suit. And he didn't want to steal that; he just wanted to buy it. He laid all his money on top of her packages and grabbed the sack she had taken from the church basement. Then he walked swiftly, quietly, hurriedly – with determination – to the door and back out into the rain.

FACING UP

J.J. was drying his hair with a towel when his grandmother got home. Having been chilled in the rain, he had even filled up the bathtub and taken a hot bath. Clean skin didn't feel half bad. Actually, it was somewhat refreshing. He sprinkled on some Cashmere Bouquet talcum power from the pink can, rubbing it around because it felt soothing. After the day he'd experienced, soothing was a good thing.

"Did you clean the tub when you finished?" Grandma Polly asked.

He threw up his arms. "There you go, ruining my bath," he said. "I was feeling so good, and you just killed it."

"The ring wouldn't be such a challenge if you took a bath more often," she said. "It's OK to be poor as long as you're clean."

J.J. rolled his eyes wondering how many times he'd heard that over the years.

She didn't suspect anything when she saw the suit hanging on the door. J.J. said he would take it to Melvin as soon as the rain stopped. She said, no, it was too late. It could wait for tomorrow.

It *was* the suit Grandma Polly had seen at the rummage sale, and she felt pleased and proud.

J. J. kept trying to swallow the lump in his throat which wouldn't go away. He didn't move when someone knocked at the door. He hid in his room until his grandmother called him.

"J.J.," she said with tears in her voice, "the sheriff is here."

Her words caught in her throat, cutting into J.J.'s heart.

He couldn't look at her when he came out of his room.

"I didn't steal it," he said without looking at the sheriff. "I left money on the chair."

"She had paid for the suit," the sheriff said. "And it wasn't yours to take even if you left money behind. You can't just walk around taking things that aren't yours. You know that's not how things work."

"How do they work?" J.J. asked. "I was doing something for a good reason."

J.J. looked at the empty spot on the door where the suit had been. There were angry voices disappearing down the stairs.

The sheriff put his arm about Grandma Polly's shoulders.

"I was doing something for someone else. I was doing something right," J.J. said, looking out the south window at the courthouse. "I keep trying to set things right."

"Your heart may have been in the right place, but your methods stink," the sheriff said.

Grandma Polly sat down by the window. She hadn't even started to cook yet which was usually her way of turning tragedy into something cope-able.

'I'm not so much angry as I am disappointed," she said.

The sheriff stood uncomfortably with his hat in his hands. "Your grandmother told me the story, and what I'm about to say next is for her, not you, and for that pitiful kid your grandma tells me you want to help. He is real, isn't he?"

"He's real."

"My kids have suits they share among them for occasions, and you can borrow one. I'll even throw in a tie. I don't have anyone in seventh grade right now who'll be going. I don't know why you couldn't just come to me in the first place, knowing the deputy and I both have a world of kids. We could dress an orphanage in hand-me-downs."

"Do you have suspenders?" J.J. asked.

"I have suspenders."

When the sheriff was gone, J.J. wanted to say something to his grandmother to make the world right, but he couldn't think of anything that would make a difference.

"Do you think I'll get my money back?" he finally whispered.

She opened her hand, showing him the money the sheriff had already returned to her. "You are the one person I've had to love for the last 13 years," she said, "and I don't want to lose you. And you took that suit from the meanest old gossip in town."

She still didn't start cooking. Supper time had passed, but she told J.J. there was some baloney in the refrigerator and a new loaf of bread. She had also brought home some strawberry shortcake from the hotel so they could celebrate the purchase of the suit at the rummage sale.

"I'm going to bed," she said. "Goodnight."

As J.J. spread Miracle Whip on a new slice of soft white Wonder Bread, he thought about heading for the sheriff's to get the suit and then on to Melvin's in the dark. But he thought better of it as he chewed on the sandwich and decided to do what he'd been told earlier, to wait until tomorrow.

He didn't touch the strawberry shortcake. He would wait for breakfast and share it with Grandma Polly. Hopefully, they could move on and laugh in the morning.

ACCEPTANCE

J.J. didn't give Melvin any peace at school, describing their plans over and over, asking Melvin to come home with him and try on the suit and shoes, new socks, and tie the sheriff had thrown in. The suit was a little big, but the shoes were fine. Melvin walked slowly to the mirror and peeked at himself, not raising his head all the way up. He leaned over to pull up his pant legs and look at his socks.

J.J. wished he would at least say the word, "socks."

"I'm sorry you can't keep the suit," J.J. said, "but the socks are yours, paid for fair and square, and I've got a little money put away so if after the dance we aren't stuffed on cake and Kool-Aid, we can go by the drug store and have a banana split or something. We may be so busy dancing with the girls we won't have a chance to get a bite of re-freshments.

"Maybe we'll even get a chance to kiss one or two of them while they're dressed up. I'm not really into that heavy yet, are you? I've promised every girl in the class a dance with me, Melvin, and I've men-tioned your name every time. There will be such a line you won't believe it. I wouldn't be surprised if some of the girls from your favorite TV program show up – Oh –you don't have a TV. Sorry I mentioned that. It doesn't matter. I don't either, but I have the hotel."

J.J. hesitated, remembering his decision not to lie to Melvin. "I made up that part about the TV personalities," he said. "There won't be anyone famous there. I'll tell you something else I've never told anyone in my life, Melvin. My father isn't famous, or if he is, I don't know about it. I don't even know who he is. Maybe people from another planet just dropped me here, because I was too short to make a good Martian. Your dad's pretty tall. Maybe you'll grow someday if you eat enough, but I will probably spend my whole life like this."

He wished Melvin would say, "Maybe your dad's tall, too. Maybe next year you'll have one of those growth spurts people talk about."

Melvin sat down on the sofa, still staring at the socks with stars in his eyes, but he nodded his head a little.

"What kind of car would you like to buy?" J. J. asked. "It's a decision we'll all have to make some day."

He took his own suit out of the closet and brushed it for the third time that same day.

Melvin stood up, going to the window, searching until he finally saw what he wanted; then he pointed across the street to the court house.

"I don't see anything but the sheriff's car," J.J. said, his eyes following where Melvin pointed.

Melvin dropped his head, but J.J. thought he was smiling. "I – I – l – li – like – the – rr-rr-red lights," he stuttered, "and the n-no-noise."

J.J. was speechless. "You really can talk!" he said. "You really can talk. Do you talk at home?"

Melvin nodded yes.

"Can you write?"

Melvin nodded again.

"Can you read?"

Melvin shook his head no.

"That's cause you're always looking at the ground," J. J. explained. "When we read in class, you need to open the books and look at the words. I'll help you. Would you like that?

Melvin nodded.

"First, you need to learn the words on the front of the stores. That's what I did," J.J. said. "The first word I ever read was 'Sears.' – I don't have many real friends. Do you, Melvin? The guys are nice to me, because I can fight and would protect them if I had to, even if I'm little. –They also don't like me because I'm mean sometimes."

Melvin shook his head yes.

The night of the dance Melvin arrived at J.J.'s door half an hour before he was expected, but J.J. had been ready since 2 p.m. His grandmother had pinned a carnation on his lapel and had one for Melvin as well.

"Mrs. Van Meter, the nice lady from the flower shop, gave them to me," she said.

J.J.'s hair was cut, and his fingers were scrubbed pink. Wherever he walked, he left a trace of aftershave spice in the air although his smooth skin had never felt a razor, at least not since he was 3-years old and an excellent climber.

Melvin had scrubbed, too, but he seemed more nervous than excited. Although his clothes were different than the usual Melvin attire, he had reverted to his old self-conscious, shrinking self. To put him at ease, J.J. continued to rattle on about all the wonderful things which were about to happen to them.

He ran out of words as they entered the front door of the rented youth building. The girls –the very same ones J.J. teased and chased as they wore skirts and matching sweater sets with white bucks and pop beads, had all become multi-colored puffs of fragrance and flowers. Their cheeks were pinked slightly with make-up, and their eyelashes were curled. Their voices were lowered, and only the familiar giggles assured J.J. they were genuinely the same girls.

Even chubby Anita looked different, wearing a white felt skirt decorated with a scatter of red fabric rosebuds which stood up away from the skirt like real flowers. The long stems, which supported the roses, continued all the way to the waist of the skirt and on up across one side of her lacy blouse. She smiled timidly at her two friends who were equally as shy as she was in the classroom, but the three of them somehow seemed collectively smitten. The trio even walked to the refreshment table together.

"Comfort buddies," J.J. thought, like him and Melvin.

If the others were surprised to see J.J. dressed in a suit, they were more surprised to see Melvin. First came the eyes, one set at a time, discovering him, and then the whispers began. For the first time Melvin was real to them. He was not an unknown in the classroom who was passed from teacher to teacher, room to room, year after year.

He was a boy in a suit going to his first dance just like all the others.

The multiple hostesses couldn't remember who had written his invitation, but it didn't matter. He had filled the formal requirement. Maybe he had a fairy godfather outside, and his transportation would turn into a pumpkin at midnight, but his dress was legitimate and acceptable. His overalls, for whatever reason, for tonight had gone "poof."

There was discussion about where he had come by his clothes. Curious eyes were on J.J., wondering what had inspired him to dress up Melvin and take him to the dance – if he in fact were the one who did it.

J.J. and Melvin visited the refreshment table, J.J. approaching the abundance with the authority of a great chef called there personally to inspect and approve of the spread.

Melvin stood with his arms behind his back as if fearful someone would smack him if he reached out; but his lips were wet, and his mouth opened with desire. His never-blinking amazed eyes were in an éclair-gaze, transfixed on the beautiful culinary wonders of the word.

There were trays of heart-shaped sandwiches with middles of rainbow colors and nutty balls of cheese surrounded by crackers of every shape. Strawberries offered two choices, chocolate covered or sugar coated. The puffy pink, yellow and green mints were topped with curly leaves and flowers, and the punch was hot or cold, a choice. There were round sugar cookies and others shaped like shells and daisies, nestled next to goodies with nuts, raisins, coconut, jelly and powdered sugar.

"Mrs. Jones," J.J. said with a bow, "is that your famous mashed potato candy? Judy brought some to the teacher this year I believe. By all means I will have to try one of those."

The deviled egg fillings lay like perfect ribbons on top of their little white boats, sprinkled with paprika and topped with –some kind of green herb? The peanuts snuggled in a silver dish with a matching spoon, allowing for delicate dipping, mixed in with almonds, walnuts and nuts as big as a grandpa's thumb.

The table itself was covered with an elegant white cloth, and two women in long dresses – more mothers? – gracefully –and some not so gracefully – lit pink candles set perfectly here and there among the dishes.

"Wow, Melvin," he whispered. "This formal idea is OK. They even trust us with fire!"

J.J. had expected there to be a record player and a stack of 45 records, but a stage had been set up with chairs, and six young men in shiny tuxedos were seated, as stately as possible, with their instruments.

The lights dimmed, and the music began, and J.J. sat down quietly with Melvin, no longer feeling brave and ready to dance with every girl in the room.

He could not think of anything to say, even to chubby Anita and her two friends. She had cheated, having turned from a self-conscious little girl into a kind-of woman with two admirers in suits to protect her. These were strange creatures, these girls in party attire with soft voices and good manners. They didn't kick the boys in the ankles the way they did at school.

On shaky stiff legs, J.J. finally stood, fixing a plate for Melvin, taking at least one of everything so that Melvin's plate pyramided, threatening dangerously to topple. There was a hole in the crystal plate for holding a punch cup, but J.J. filled it with deviled eggs, carrying Melvin a cup of punch in his other hand.

"You have to try it all, Melvin," he said. "This is our big night. As soon as you finish the punch, if you want to try the other one, I'll get it for you. Or if you get to feelin' a little braver, you can go filler-up yourself. And if you need to pee, you just tell me, Melvin, and I'll show you the bathrooms. I'll take care of you, Melvin. Don't worry about a thing."

J.J. picked up a plate for himself at the enormous table of edibles and marveled a second time that the plates were not paper or chipped china like at the hotel. He watched two mothers in long dresses, wondering if they would put on long aprons later to *worsch* dishes.

He didn't know what to choose for his own refreshments, wanting to try it all, just as he had instructed Melvin. He kept a sophisticated air about him, shaking his head occasionally as if dismissing one treat, changing his mind, choosing it and another as well. His plate was almost as full as Melvin's, but he chose the hot punch for himself.

"I had something very like this once when in Washington, D.C., he said to Toni's beautiful red-haired mother. "My father was a senator before his death and would likely have run for president if he hadn't been hit by a train."

As Melvin and J.J. ate their tiny sandwiches and bakery cookies, J.J. talked less boldly than before but kept chattering with never-ending enthusiasm, trying to boost Melvin's morale, grateful he had Melvin to watch after. Without him, J.J. realized he would have long before, without even tasting a sandwich, run out, making a get-away, finding a bush to hide behind where he could watch without being part of it.

After a great deal of self-preaching, he asked a girl to dance although he had no idea how to dance. Somehow, with the business of finding Melvin a suit, J.J. had forgotten about learning to dance. He was upset he hadn't taken up chubby Anita's offer that they practice with her two friends. He wondered if the trio had indeed practiced. She danced with one and then the other. They didn't move much, but they weren't nervous.

J.J. tried pulling a girl onto the dance floor with all the cool Uncle Fred may have used, and to his surprise, she reacted well. He put one arm around her waist, wondering why he had never noticed before how fragile and narrow girls are in that area. She must have been from the "other" seventh-grade class because he didn't recognize her, and he was pretty sure with his reputation, if she knew who he was, she wouldn't have agreed to dance with him.

Looking around, he saw some of the girls laying their heads on the shoulders of the boys, trying to look so in love. He was grateful he was too short, so that no girl could put her head on his shoulder without getting a crick in her neck.

J.J. didn't talk as he followed his partner's feet about the floor, but he did notice the sweetness of soap and perfume and looked at her little pink ears with rhinestone stars dangling from them. He studied the weensy curls which were left at the nape of her neck after her long hair had been pulled up on top of her head. She was so much a girl it was creepy.

"It's OK. I don't mind leading," she said. She gave him an, "I like you," smile, and he tried again to remember her name.

When the dance ended, she kept his hand, not letting him get away to keep his promise to dance with every girl there. He melted in obedience, not out of devotion, because it made life simple. At the same time, her capture of him meant he didn't have to find someone else to dance with. Then again, how would he get rid of her later? What was she expecting? What message had he delivered when he'd asked her to dance? He hadn't intended to send any message at all, but he got the feeling she had received one.

Melvin had not danced but sat in the dim light, staring at the dance floor in wonder, his eyes open, his body still shrinking. Had he even blinked?

J.J. waved, but Melvin didn't notice. He was in another zone.

What was going through his mind?

Was he listening to the music?

Did he want to run away?

J.J. himself didn't want to dance with any of the popular girls except Julia. Everyone wanted to dance with Julia although she had a boyfriend.

The other girls made his stomach roll the same way it did when he ate ice cream on a hot summer day and then went running in the sun. It didn't make any difference anyway. The girl who was holding his hand had ended any plans he had for moving on.

His mind wandered. Were girls' cheeks as soft as they looked? Their lips were off limits but intriguing.

He could never have predicted what happened next.

No one could.

In years to come he might even ask himself why she did it.

What she did was so very kind, and it took courage, real courage.

The "she" in this instance was Toni, wearing an elegant black sheath dress and high heels.

An Italian beauty, she shooed away other pursuers and walked to Melvin, setting his plate aside, pulling him up to his feet, letting him know that his reward for existing was to dance with one of the number-one girls in their grade.

She was in fact even one of the party hostesses with her mother. She may have even been the one who wrote his invitation. Melvin, without asking, had been given the ultimate stamp of approval, in so many words had been truly knighted.

Melvin followed Toni onto the dance floor in disbelief, putting one arm around her waist like J.J. had told him on the way to the dance.

J.J. was so proud – and envious.

The music began, and Toni smiled, trying to show Melvin what to do, trying to make him feel comfortable.

She didn't make fun; she tried to be helpful.

Almost the entire universe froze to watch Toni dance with the suited nobody.

No punch was poured.

No other feet moved.

Nothing came out of the kitchen.

Time stopped.

J.J. saw emotion building up in Melvin, his face growing from skeleton white to humiliated on-a-stage pink, to red, to increasingly red,

raging red,

stop-the-world red,

center-of-the earth red,

dying-boiling-let-me-out-of-here red.

Melvin's face looked like a setting on a machine that any minute would explode, bursting into volcanic metal that would spray the universe.

J.J. thought of the donut mechanism where he had lunch sometimes. Normally, the donuts just kept rolling and rolling and rolling and rolling and rolling; but if it had gone as awry as Melvin looked now, donuts would have POW-ed out like bullets, hitting the ceiling and walls; batter would have mushed its way onto the counters in blobs, and people would have run out the doors, screaming with fear, having seen the happy donut maker gone crazy.

Sweat poured down Melvin's face – and in sympathy, J.J.'s own body.

J.J. clinched and unclenched his fists in fear for his friend, wondering if he had abandoned him too soon.

It had seemed all right to leave Melvin there to watch, but then that miracle happened, and Melvin was on his feet, dancing with one of the most beautiful girls in the room.

Melvin's head suddenly dropped lower than dirt, and his feet stopped almost as if he had clamped them to the hardwood floor.

Melvin was stunned, apparently unconscious without knowing what to do next. Things looked OK for a while, but it had become too real. This was not a world Melvin understood.

J.J. fought to understand but was not sure that he did.

After being a non-person for 13 years, Melvin had been accepted, even if just for a few minutes.

Melvin was, J.J. thought, a boy Cinderella for real, but the clock was striking twelve, and he was terrified.

Melvin's body began to shake, frail as it was.

He lifted his hands to his face to brush away the tears which wouldn't stop, and there he stood in the middle of the dance floor with every eye watching as he began to sob out loud, streams of water trickling down his cheeks, garbled cries, muffled only by the thunder of the music.

As he ran out of the ballroom, leaving Toni alone on the dance floor, J. J. took off in a run after him, and the two started up the dark street towards town.

No one ran after them.

It was O.K.

The chilly breeze which came over them was a blessing, a new beginning, a chance to start this night all over.

J.J. was again relieved he had taken on Melvin as a responsibility. It had given him a chance to leave the dance as well and to get away from the girl whose name he didn't even know who seemed to have kisses in her eyes.

In no time at all she may have laid her head on his shoulder and got a crick in her neck.

"I'm sorry, Melvin," J.J. began after a long silence.

"They hurt you, didn't they? You thought they were making fun of you. They weren't, Melvin! With God as my witness, you were accepted! You made it! They wanted you to feel part of the magic. If there were a golden circle to grab, Melvin, you grabbed it. Tears or not, you did this! You were a success!"

J.J. shook his head in disbelief. "For the rest of your life you can remember the night you were pulled onto the dance floor by a beautiful woman. Honestly, Melvin, I don't expect that ever to happen to me. But I'm grateful it happened to you."

Melvin shook his head no, reaching into one pocket, showing J. J. a sandwich he had carefully wrapped in a white napkin decorated with pink and blue daisies. In the other pocket he had a selection of colored cookies and salty multi-kind nuts. Most cherished seemed to be several soft butter mints with flowers on top which he had in his inside suit pocket.

"You really take the cake," J.J. said, laughing in the chilly spring air. "Did you hear what I said? Get it? You really did take the cake!

"Got any punch?" J. J. asked, faking the next laugh, trying to cheer up Melvin.

"Let me guess," he continued. "You thought it was New York, Hollywood and heaven all rolled into one."

Melvin nodded.

"So why are you crying? Are you happy? If I'd had Toni in my arms, I wouldn't have let go until at least I smacked a big one on her!"

Melvin hesitated in his steps and looked up, giving J.J. a questionable look. Melvin was challenging him, although quietly, to put his cards on the table.

"OK, so I wouldn't have done that," J.J. confessed, "but you were livin' my dream, Man! Were those tears of joy?

Melvin nodded again, taking off his borrowed tie and handing it to J.J.

"B-ba-but – tomorrow," he whispered.

"But tomorrow," J.J. repeated to himself.

But tomorrow.

Tomorrow the suit would go back to the sheriff along with the tie. The girls would go back to their sweaters, pop beads, and white bucks and kicking the boys in the ankles. Why? Because boys are not allowed to kick and hit back.

Melvin would be back at the shack with his new socks and the cracks in the wall.

He had joined the world and had a taste of humanity, but the dance had ended for him, and he would be expected to get back on the shelf, his hole in the wall, his nothingness."

Would Toni's sweet deed become just part of the past as well? Come Monday, would for some of the boys turn it into a joke, envious they had not been the one chosen?

J.J. hoped not.

But like before, nothing would be expected of Melvin.

He would merely exist.

Nothing had really changed.

What they had planned for weeks had come and gone.

"Well, Melvin," J.J. said, "you could have left one of your shoes back there when you ran out, and the mayor could hire somebody to find the boy it fit. They could at least buy you a hamburger or something for having the winning shoe.

"Let's make the night last as long as we can."

Suddenly, a smile covered J.J.'s face.

He undid his tie, and the April breeze found his neck.

"I just remembered!" he said.

"SPEAKING OF SHOES, YOU GET TO KEEP THE SHOES!"

When they passed the hotel, J.J. pulled Melvin inside and ordered Cokes and fries, putting his money on the counter, knowing it would be enough. He had, after all, not had to buy the suit. The sheriff saw that he got the money back he had left for the meanest old gossip in town.

J.J.'s Coke glass had a lipstick smudge on the edge when it was set before him, but he wiped it off with a napkin and didn't complain.

"I'm going to remember this night, Melvin," J.J. said thoughtfully as they chewed on the ends of the fries after dipping them in catsup.

Melvin nodded a me-too, kind of nod. He had a dictionary of nods.

"Seems to me we ought to be able to do something, Melvin. Everyone ought to have something they can do, a spot where they fit?

" Did you see those girls, Melvin? You didn't feel like you fit in really, did you? I didn't either.

"But those that looked like they fit in -- well, they were just better pretenders than we are. None of them had been to a party like that before either. None of them, even the girls with their big dotted i's and fancy invitations.

"Let's always be friends, Melvin. I been helping you learn to read. You can show me how to – what can you do, Melvin?"

Melvin reached into the inside pocket of his borrowed suit, where his treasured mints were melting, pulling out a piece of wood, the top of which was beginning to look like the head of a dog.

J. J. whistled. "You can whittle!" he shouted. "And you can whittle good. I didn't think anyone could whittle anymore, Melvin. When you grow up, the magazines can write stories about how you come from this small town and restarted whittling. Maybe they'll even write a song about you. They'll probably say it was a lost art until you came along and found it again. You could be famous, Melvin. And I could tell everyone I knew you when Toni picked you out to dance with her at the party, you in particular over all the other boys."

Silence.

Silence.

Painful silence.

"I always wished I had a dog, Melvin."

There was something final about the sound of his voice as if he knew it would never happen.

Melvin stopped by J.J.'s to drop off the suit, and they transported Melvin's array of party treats first into individual napkins and then into an empty bread sack.

"I hope you give that mint to your sweet little sister," J.J. said as he helped prepare the goody bag for Melvin's siblings, adding a few choice bits from his own pockets.

After walking with Melvin to the lake shack, feeling no fear, J.J. sat down on the step in front of the drug store which had closed some time ago. Nothing was stirring. It was still too early – for even mosquitoes.

He listened to the few night noises of the square, a car passing now and then, the clock striking the hour and dinging the half hour, the rustle of bird's wings in the gutters.

Grandma wasn't at the hotel, so she must have been asleep, he thought. He would be careful not to wake her, although there was a lot to share --

He wasn't startled when he saw a man coming down the street, believing for the moment he didn't have an enemy in the world. He was ready to call out a friendly *hello*, but then the figure started to look more familiar.

"It's time," the man said. "We need for you that little favor."

All the beauty of the evening dissipated. J.J.'s eyes filled with horror.

ATTACKED

J.J. tried to hide his bruised face from Grandma Polly, but it was impossible. For every bruise he could hide, there were 10 more. The sheriff looked sympathetic, but J.J. knew there could really be trouble.

"Who beat you up, J.J.?" the sheriff asked.

J.J. sat on the side of a hospital bed, having dressed to go home. He had been unconscious when he'd been taken to the hospital, and he'd been kept there overnight for what he remembered later as x-rays, patching and preaching.

"We all know it wasn't a kid, because there's not a kid in town who could beat you up," Sheriff Doolin half ranted.

"Those bruises on your face were made by a grown man – or a baseball bat. Your jaw and nose are broken for Pete's sake. This is exactly the reason I tell you not to be walking all over the town like you own the place. As sweet as some people can be, there are mean ones out there! There's more to this than you're telling me."

"I'm not protecting anyone out of loyalty," J.J. said, hurting so many places he thought being dead might be a relief. "The man who did this said they'd kill me if I told."

He reached out to pat his grandmother but winced with the gesture. "And they threatened to hurt my grandma. I know I've told stories in the past, Sheriff. I've spun some yarns. But this is true."

"I believe you," the sheriff said, pacing while rubbing the back of his head with his hand.

"Why did they do it, J.J.?" "Why would they break your arm? I hate to think we have people like that in this good little town."

"They were upset I wouldn't help them with some kind of break-in," J.J. said. "He said I was small enough to crawl through a hole and let them in."

"Well, which is it, *he* or *they*?" the sheriff demanded.

"Only one talked to me, but he said there were others," J.J. explained.

"I said from the beginning I wouldn't do it. I was scared for a couple days, but I got so excited about the dance and helping Melvin learn to read, I just forgot to look over my shoulder. I was so relieved the whole suit thing was settled. Those last days before the dance were like a vacation. I just pretended the danger wasn't real."

The sheriff threw up his hands in defeat and told Grandma Baskin to take J.J. home. "I don't think *they'll* bother him anymore," he said, "or *he* won't bother J.J. any more. I don't know who we're looking for or how many. Until he's ready to point *them* – *him* – out, my hands are tied."

Grandma clutched a paper bag in her hands, and J.J. knew it was a bag of rags which used to be his cherished suit. Marks from the tie were on his throat as if he had been choked before he was let go.

J.J. walked his grandmother to the hotel but didn't go home, although she and the sheriff both had said he should go straight home and go to bed.

He kept up as steady a pace as he was able until he got to school, checking in late at the office. There were whispers as he limped down the hallway and found his place in the classroom.

He gave Gene a cold look when he saw him, and Gene looked away, more scared than embarrassed, knowing more than the others what had happened. He didn't look any happier as if his dad had come home with a pot load of money."

J.J. wasn't upset with Melvin. There was no reason to be. Melvin hadn't said he had to walk to the lake with him. But in the past few weeks, as they became better friends, and Melvin's father became more trusting of J.J. ,he felt he had to make sure Melvin got home safely. And truthfully, Melvin was safely home when J.J. was kid-napped.

They'd had a good week leading up to the dance.

J.J. kept telling Melvin he had to look up and get his book out in class if he wanted to learn to read. Melvin seemed to be picking up words and sounding things out pretty fast, as if he had been learning all that time he sat in class like a mummy. J.J. had just pulled the cork, and the words started spilling out – slowly.

Until J.J. started trying to teach Melvin, he hadn't known he was such a good reader himself. Grandma Polly had started reading to him years ago. He read his first storybook on her lap.

But when his turn came to read in class, he always said, "I pass," so he could keep up his tough guy image.

Melvin had been sliding by all those years, and making new habits is not easy. He would in fact have to "own up" that he could do things before anything got done.

Everyone stared when J.J. walked into class.

J.J.'s right eye was swollen shut, and he almost cried as he reached to touch his cheek where the stitches pulled. His tongue tried to soothe the bloody hole inside his mouth where his left eye tooth had been – and the tooth next to it. His elbow ached where the bone had been shattered.

Melvin sneaked a peek at J.J. out of the corner of his eyes and then reached into his desk and took out his book, opening it.

He smiled a little as if to say, "Look what I'm doing."

J.J. used his good arm to pull the literature text book out of his own desk as well, but he was in too much pain to hold it open and find the right page. His broken ribs throbbed when he tried to adjust himself in his seat. He gasped, thinking for a moment he would pass out; and the others watched him like a quiet creature with 50 eyes and 25 noses.

For the first time in his life, he was really frightened. He was afraid Gene's dad and his friends would return to finish the job. And he admittedly wanted to be with the other kids. He wanted to see them in their everyday clothes and remember all the fun they'd been having just a few hours before he was beaten up.

Melvin raised his eyes to the teacher as if waiting for her approval.

Who would know she could read his mind?

She nodded.

Seeing he would not be in trouble, he scooted his desk next to J.J.'s with a screech and then reached over to open J.J.'s book.

He flipped to Page 48 where they had left off, looking carefully at the numbers to make sure he'd found the right page.

J.J.'s mind was too foggy to realize what was happening.

He had never really figured there was any point in trying to teach Melvin to read.

There had to have been some reason the teachers gave up on him years ago – in first grade even.

During their after-school sessions, J.J. liked the spot of light which came into Melvin's eyes when J.J. stopped reading to explain parts of the stories.

J.J. so loved to pretend he had been places and seen things. If they read about oranges, J.J. told Melvin about how they grew on trees and how good they smelled. If they read about a state, J.J. got out the free Atlas he'd been given by an insurance man, and they looked the state up to see what shape it was.

This day on J.J.'s return to school, the students read out loud, one after the other, and J.J. tried to listen although his chest ached, and his arm throbbed, not missing a nerve.

The principal would probably give him a ride home, which would be OK because he didn't want to be alone.

The faces which surrounded him were suddenly cherished and vital.

A tear sneaked out of his eye, and he reached up to destroy the sissy evidence before anyone saw it.

His pain was intense, but he was embarrassed to be hurt enough to cry – hurt inside and out.

He had made the best decision.

He had told Gene's drunken father *no.*

He had done the right thing, and look what happened.

Everything hurt – his trust, his pride, his soul.

Mrs. Franks saw the tear and opened her mouth as if to ask him a question, but she seemed to think better of it. "Who wants to read next?" she asked. She was probably thinking what he knew already, that he should be at home.

J.J.'s mind whirled with misery, and loneliness flooded through him.

He longed for a different world to be part of something better.

He wanted to know what J. J. stood for.

He was tired of wandering the streets trying to make a little money, smiling when nothing was funny, and having to fight his way along to get anything.

Why didn't he have a father to help him fight back?

How he hated that non-existent father!

Almost as soon as he had the thought, he looked straight at Gene and felt sorry for him.

Gene had a father – but then again, did he? Was there just a mean man who lived in Gene's house making everyone's life miserable?

And then it happened.

Melvin, although shrunk low in his desk which he had scooted up next to J.J.'s desk, raised his hand ever-so-slightly.

The class stopped breathing.

It was as if they shared one collective lung, and it had gone as flat as a tire running over a broken bottle.

"Would you like to read, Melvin?" Mrs. Franks asked, although her voice cracked a little.

J.J. figured she would cry when she got home, thinking, "Melvin read today."

Melvin shook his head yes.

"We would all love to hear you read, Melvin," she continued. "Go ahead."

J.J. concentrated on Melvin, trying to listen, to remember the dance, the suit, the fancy sandwiches and the good feeling he had in trying to help his friend.

The class strained to hear; the collective lung was on hold, and everyone leaned over in anticipation.

"Ba-ba-Benny Za-Za-Zimmerman -- Ra-ra-Ross sha-sha-shouted, ree-ree-realizing Ta-ta-Thomas may have ha-ha-heard," Melvin read.

"He pa-peeked over his sha-sha shoulder t-t-t-towards the d-d-door. The co-co-counselor sa-sa-saw the g-g—ga-glance. 'Is the gho-gho-ghost ow-ow-out there?' he ah-ah-asked."

Melvin traced along the words with his finger as he read, and Mrs. Franks put her hand over her mouth, obviously holding back emotion, not asking him to stop. His reading was boringly slow, and he stopped frequently to think out even simple words; but she didn't want to break the spell mid-stress.

The class grew restless quickly as the surprise of the reading-Melvin miracle wore off, but Melvin continued, looking from time to time at J.J., wanting as best he could, make his friend feel better, to take his pain away, to do for J.J. what J.J. had tried to do for him.

Melvin's face kept growing redder, perspiration was pouring down his neck, but he didn't cry like at the dance. He read on, trying to comfort his hurting friend.

The boredom of the painful reading broke when the sheriff appeared in the doorway, motioning for J.J.

No!

J.J. stood up so slowly that Melvin stood up, too, helping him on one side. Ron, although on crutches himself from an accident, got out of his seat as well and supported him from the other.

J.J. didn't complain about their fussing. As they helped him walk to the door, he figured the sheriff had more questions he would refuse to answer.

Gene put his head on his desk and covered it with his hands. If he had crawled under his desk, he would have been in the duck-and-cover position the kids had learned to do if there were ever a bomb dropped.

J.J. reached with his good arm to pat Melvin on the shoulder as he left the room, and he intended to give Gene a goodbye glare but was touched when he saw that Gene was in pain, too, another kind of pain.

He was amazed somewhat when the sheriff put his arms around him in – a daddy hug of sorts.

Yes, it was, really, a daddy kind of hug.

J.J. had seen other kids get those hugs, but not from the sheriff. "You stubborn little so-in-so," the sheriff said. "How did you ever get to school on your own? You're supposed to be at home in bed."

"I walked. I fell. I rested," said J.J. "I may have slept a little. I didn't know I could walk that far with no one driving by. Not one soul drove by."

His words were slurred as they came from his swollen blue lips.

The sheriff scooped J.J. up in his arms and carried him out to the squad car. They rode in silence back to the sheriff's office.

The sheriff didn't say anything right away when they got inside. He unwrapped a Baby Ruth candy bar, broke it in half and handed half to J.J. The sheriff took a bite, soon realizing J.J. wouldn't be able to eat his half. The kind gesture turned uncomfortable.

"I have some cold 7-Up," he said. "You want a 7-Up?"

Getting the 7-Up gave them both excuse not to say anything.

J.J. took the icy bottle with his good hand, pressing it gently against his forehead, minding not to touch the sensitive stitches.

"Did you ever notice Butterfingers are kind of splintery?" J.J. asked, not seeming to be aiming the question at anyone.

"They're my favorite actually."

He closed his eyes because talking was painful.

"I'm sorry I didn't know that," the sheriff said. "I would have bought that instead of the Baby Ruth, and it would have been softer. We could have let it warm up a bit first."

J.J. had never realized how many places there were in a face that could hurt, and he hated the taste of blood. He was embarrassed to realize he was slobbering a little where his mouth wouldn't close.

Seeing that the bottle was difficult for him to drink from, the sheriff got a cup, took the bottle back, set the cup on the desk and poured slowly.

The fizzy bubbles sounded loud.

"This cup will make it a little easier for you to drink," the sheriff said quietly. "Get a little in you if you can. You need the liquid."

J.J. tilted his head back and poured some of the 7-Up into the narrow opening between his lips, grateful for the cold drink which soothed at the same time it took some of the bloody taste away, not entirely, but enough.

He burped but winced because even that hurt.

"I told you I can't tell you who beat me up," J.J. began. "But I'm glad you got me out of class, because I don't feel so good, and Melvin's reading was a bit much. I just want to go home, lock the door, and sleep."

The sheriff stood up, coughed, and leaned over to give J.J. another hug, but J.J. cried out in pain, so he pulled away, sorry.

"You are acting so creepy," J.J. mumbled.

The sheriff fell back down in his chair and leaned forward, his hands clenched together in front of him, resting on the desk.

"I didn't go to the school to question you," the sheriff said. "No matter what you may think, I even like you. This is the hardest job I have ever had in my whole life. J.J. – it's your grandma."

"Did she get hurt?" J.J. asked, trying desperately to see the sheriff through swollen eyes. He stood up, trembling. He didn't feel strong any more. He just wanted to be a little boy. Did those jerks beat up his grandma?

"No, J.J., she had a heart attack at the hotel while she was at work," the sheriff answered gently.

"But she's all right? I can go see her in the hospital? I can start doing more around the house! I won't worry her so much! We can find Uncle Fred and pay the hospital, Sheriff. We can pay, and they can make her well."

"Remember you aren't doing so well yourself. The doctor was right there, J.J. You know how he liked your grandmother a lot, and he worked over her. He did everything he knew how, used every trick he could remember. He worked a long time. He's good. But he's not good enough to combat a massive coronary. J.J., your grandmother is gone. If it's possible, I think the doctor was in more disbelief than you are."

"It's my fault," J.J. said. "I did it to her. It's the things I let happen to me."

He moved, restlessly, but with misery, a rhythm of pain, inside and out. He wanted to cry, but it just made the physical pain worse.

"No," the sheriff said. "It wasn't your fault. I knew you'd be asking that, so I spoke to the doctor, and he said it was time. It would have happened no matter what. She was tired. And if the beating upset her, that wasn't your fault. It was the fault of the men who did it. I'll see that you're safe. There are two reasons I want to know who did this, J.J. I want to arrest them – or him, and I don't want anyone else to be hurt like you. You're not the only kid in town your age small enough to crawl through a hole and unlock a door."

J.J. hadn't thought of that. What if they had wanted scrawny little ol' Melvin to crawl through a hole and open a door?

"Did they offer to pay you?" the sheriff asked. "Did he offer to pay you?"

"A couple thousand dollars," J.J. replied.

"You do realize these kinds of people don't know what it is to be fair or generous. They don't share, and they wouldn't have left behind a witness. Do you agree?"

Melvin's face passed through J.J.'s mind. A lot of faces came to mind, all of them as small or smaller than he.

"It was Gene's dad," he said finally.

The day had been a tough one. He wasn't sure he wanted to ask the next question.

"Is my uncle coming to live with me?" J.J. asked, not really wanting the answer he was pretty sure he would get. "He lives with us some-times, you know. He's not much, but I guess he's all I got left."

"We don't know where he is," the sheriff said. "But we're trying to look. When did you see him last?"

J.J.'s head sunk between his knees, Melvin-like, his eyes concentrating on a coffee stain in the carpet; he didn't say anything for a minute, knowing what would be coming next.

"I haven't seen him in a while," he said finally. "He likes to go up North fishing. He likes the rodeo circuit. He likes New Orleans. I'm pretty sure he rides empty box cars on the trains. He's never been much for roots – or postcards."

The sheriff's cough was a bad sign something uncomfortable was coming.

"A lady from the county will be here to get you in a bit, J.J. She's coming here to the office. Someone will get your things for you. This may turn out better than you think. Don't worry. You might have a family with a dad to help you out when you get in a stew. Maybe you'll be in a family with other kids, brothers and sisters."

"What if they don't like me?" J. J. asked. "Do you think they'll have a dog?"

He sniffed, moving his foot back and forth over the coffee stain. "What will they think of a kid with no name? Why can't I live with you? Why can't the doctor take me? I could help him a lot. Call Ben at the liquor store. Maybe he wants me."

HOME AT LAST

J.J. didn't recognize his uncle at first. He hadn't seen him in three months. And he didn't speak when Uncle Fred first came through the door.

They sat in the summer heat on the front porch of the house where J.J. lived, staring out over the street. Some children passed on bicycles and waved, and the ice cream truck was somewhere in the distance, close enough they could hear the bell.

"Do you like it here?" Uncle Fred asked. "The folks seem real nice." He fidgeted, trying to get comfortable.

"It's OK," J.J. said. "They've got two kids of their own, and they've got three extras like me. My foster dad is OK. He's strict, but strict isn't all that bad. He's having me save my money so that in four years when I get my license, I can buy a car, maybe not a new Thunderbird convertible like I want but something with wheels that runs on gas. He doesn't let anyone hurt me. He takes up for me when I'm right."

J.J. still refused to look at his uncle. His face had healed, and his teeth were repaired, better than before actually. He rubbed his arm, still in pain sometimes. The doctor in his new town said it would take time to be 100 percent again.

"It's good having someone look out for you," Uncle Fred said.

"You're probably charming them, and they sound practical. You still selling cocktail wieners for money?"

J.J. shrugged, walked down the steps and picked up a stick so he could draw in the dirt. "I'm 20 miles away from my hometown. I can't get to the liquor store for meats any more. I lost my supplier so to speak, and the Mrs. in there would throw a fit if I went in a liquor store –my new mom. But Ben sent word he's closed the liquor store anyway and opened a deli in a department store. He's doing fine with it, too, calls it Ben's Party Peppers and Pickles.

"My foster mom said I could sell other things –greeting cards, wrapping paper and stuff, and I put some of that money away for my car. My new dad is teaching me how to work on cars, too, so some day I can make a little money with that. I'm doing OK."

He smiled a little.

"Sheriff comes to visit. He says I'm going to be a gall-darned attorney."

"Well, sometimes I could use your help there," his uncle said softly. "Would I have to pay you full price?"

There was a chilling silence.

"J.J., there's no chance of our getting together. I had to tell you that in person. I was always the bad apple of the family, and my life isn't anything for a boy with possibilities. Your grandma, my mother, always thought you would grow up to be a good businessman if you had some guidance and didn't end up in jail first." He tried to laugh, but it wasn't funny.

J.J. nodded. "Did you hear me askin' for anything? Did I ever ask you for anything? You didn't see me run for my suitcase as soon as you came to the door. I know from experience what to expect from you."

Uncle Fred got up and walked out in the yard to light a cigarette, not liking reminders he was worthless.

"But before you do," J. J. ventured, "with Grandma gone now, if you don't tell me who I am, I'll never know."

He held his breath, waiting. "I have to know, Fred."

"Fred? What happened to uncle?" the answer came.

"If you were my uncle, you'd be planning a home for us," J.J. said. "You haven't earned the title. If I call anyone uncle again, it will likely be the sheriff or Ben. Maybe when I'm 16, I'll drive back and forth and work for Ben, or maybe I'll have a place of my own by then."

Uncle Fred took out some chewing gum — Blackjack – which looked just like it sounded and tasted like licorice. He fingered the blue package thoughtfully. He sat down and started moving the porch swing back and forth, resting back on his heels and then sticking his legs out in front of him to pump.

"Someone should have told you," he said. "I'm sorry, J.J. Your grandmother was afraid. Your grandfather was a soldier, and even though he was wounded, the military meant a lot to him. When your daddy and I were growing up, he wanted us to be military, too.

"Your grandpa preached to us a lot. But we were peaceful little guys like your grandma, at least compared to him. They put a lot of store in your daddy because he did well in school, and they had high hopes for him. I don't know that anyone ever made any plans for me or had any hopes. There are kids like me, the ones who get lost in the shuffle."

"Or who don't have any interest in being part of the shuffle," J.J. interrupted.

Uncle Fred almost laughed. "You've got me figured out, don't you? There's no buttering you up with sympathy."

"Your grandpa was convinced that if your father were in the military, he could handle every world problem that came up. Your dad had his eye on college, but knowing how your grandpa felt, he gave in.

He'd been dating this girl with pretty big brown eyes and dark brunette curls. I used to wish she were mine. Your dad always got anything worth having. He ran off and married her without telling anyone. I think he was afraid the folks wouldn't like her, and there'd be another hassle.

"She got really upset when she found out your dad joined the Navy, and she said she didn't want to have anything more to do with him or anything that had to do with him if he planned to leave her alone and go off on a ship. She said if he had any spine, he'd not let his father choose his career for him. She took drastic action. She left you with your father, and he brought you home. Your grandpa died, your dad was killed in an accident aboard ship, and your grandmother thought everything she ever loved was gone except for you."

"You expected me to guess all that?"

"Your grandma left Nebraska with you, moved to the apartment over the drug store, and got the hotel job, thinking if she were in some small town, your mother would never find you.

"She didn't want anyone to know who you were for sure. She even saw me as a threat. That's why I never stayed around much. She knew I thought she should look for your mother, tell her your dad was dead and ask her if she wanted you. It was the right thing to do, and she loved you too much to do the right thing. She used to look at any missing children stories in the newspaper as if they were rattlesnakes, always fearful some little baby picture of you would show up and someone would recognize you."

"So, I really have a mother?" J.J. asked. "And do you think I could think of my father as a hero? Do you have a picture? Was she really beautiful?"

"She was," Uncle Fred said. "I don't know where she is, but I am looking all over the country. I'll keep my eyes open. By now she's probably sorry she left you behind. I'll bet she's looking for you, wondering what you look like. She wasn't the kind to run out on a baby like that. I think she figured if she did something drastic enough like leave you with your dad and run off, he'd go get her. And I think he likely would have eventually if he hadn't been killed."

Uncle Fred looked at his watch. "I've got a bus to catch," he said, pulling out his wallet, searching until he found an old photograph hidden under an expired I.D. He handed it to J.J. "That's your dad on the left. You can hardly tell us apart, but he looks confident."

J.J. took it reverently, almost afraid to look.

"I'm sorry. I had a picture of your mom, too, but I got drunk every time I looked at it, so I tore it up. I tore it up and taped it back together three times actually. Finally, it just wouldn't repair anymore. I loved her, J.J. You'll never know how much I loved her. The picture's gone, but I see her every night in my mind and heart just as clear as if she were right here. So, I think of her and get drunk now."

"It's funny how you always have a bus to catch when you say you aren't' headed anywhere," J.J. said.

"Don't leave without telling me what my name is." He sat down in the porch swing, happier somehow. He had quit rubbing his aching arm to stare at the picture.

"You may not want to know. You were named for your father first of all. Your first name is rightfully Joseph," Uncle Fred shared.

"And my middle name?" J.J. asked, leaning forward eagerly.

"Well, your mom and dad wanted to name you equally for both parents. Your whole name is Joseph Jane Baker. Your grandmother changed her name and yours. It could have been worse."

"Jane?" J.J. shouted. "My middle name is Jane?"

Uncle Fred threw up his arms in helplessness. "Don't look at me! I was the black sheep! No one asked my opinion."

He pointed at J.J. as if he had just remembered something.

"I dropped by the sheriff's office to find out where you were," he continued, reaching into his pocket. "And on his desk, he had a little something from a friend of yours. So, the sheriff comes by to see you? Huh? Friendly visits. He's plum out of anything to do with you gone. There are no short-legged tikes selling cocktail meats on the street or cards with necked ladies on the front. The junior high is a quart low on chewin' tobacco, and they tell me no one's nabbed a suit to pass on to a poor boy in some time."

He grinned.

"Ah! Here it is!" he shouted, holding out a small wooden dog which had been carefully carved and polished. On the bottom were the initials M.B.

"There's a note, too," Uncle Fred continued, handing him a small dirty piece of paper.

"A note from Melvin?" J.J. yelled. "A note from Melvin? I don't believe it!"

"To J.J. my friend," the note began. "Here's the dog you wanted. Thank you. Your friend, Melvin Beasley. P.S. They made me go to summer school."

Uncle Fred had walked to the edge of the sidewalk by now, and J.J. looked up to watch him go, trying to be only half interested, opening his mouth to call out but thinking of nothing worthwhile to say.

It was true. Uncle Fred had no life to offer anyone. J.J. didn't want to be a bum. He wanted to be somebody.

After all, he was a man with a name. His dad was a hero who had died on a ship, probably saving someone's life.

J.J. sat under the tree in the backyard for a long time. His foster mother peeked out, smiled when she saw that everything was OK, but asked no questions.

J.J. looked at the little dog – some kind of spaniel maybe. It didn't look like Melvin's skinny old dog.

J. J. clutched the dog, repeating to himself over and over, "Joseph J. Baker. I'm Joseph J. Baker."

He got up, making his way to the kitchen, waiting until his new family looked up in unison to make his announcement.

'Hi," he said, "I'm Joseph J. Baker."

They smiled but didn't respond.

"No," he said. "In respect for my mother –ahem –I am Joseph Jane Baker. That's not one of my stories. That's a fact."

No one laughed.

DROP-OUT

By Jo-Ann Jennings

It was kicking leaves time,
And you didn't care a whole lot
That they itch when they got
Stuck down your coat,
But you cared a little bit.
There was smoke in the air,
Not bad, but hinting at
Football games and crisp air
And the first day of school.
The classroom smelled of
New leather
New erasers
New fabric
Furniture polish
Pencils
And Cashmere Bouquet bath powder.
And there was that boy again
Who came back every year
To sit with his head down
And his back bent, not seeing
Or hearing
It would seem
Any of the wonders
That I felt and saw.
I would grow up,
But one day

Between eighth grade
And ninth
He would be just be
Swallowed up by a desk.
I don't know –
But I'm pretty sure.